Tales from Devana High

Concrete Chips

Tales from Devana High
Concrete Chips

Bali Rai

Hodder
Children's
Books

A division of Hodder Headline Limited

A Catalogue record for this book is available from
the British Library

ISBN 0 340 87728 6

Typeset in Garamond by Avon DataSet Ltd,
Bidford-on-Avon, Warwickshire

Printed and bound in Great Britain by
Bookmarque Ltd, Croydon, Surrey

The paper and board used in this paperback are natural recyclable
products made from wood grown in sustainable forests.
The manufacturing processes conform to the environmental
regulations of the country of origin.

Hodder Children's Books
A division of Hodder Headline Limited
338 Euston Road
London NW1 3BH

To everyone who attended
Judgemeadow 1983–1988.
Even the teachers . . .

ONE

'Come on Grace! You're going to be late . . .'

I groaned and turned my head, pulling the pillow over it. My bed was so warm.

'Grace . . .'

I looked out from under my pillow.

'Urrggh . . .' I groaned.

'Grace!'

Just ten more minutes. Just ten, I thought. The world wasn't going anywhere, was it? Stinky school could wait . . .

'Get up you lazy little . . .'

This time Dad's voice was right outside my bedroom door. I blinked at the light coming in through the blinds and groaned again before slipping a leg out of bed to test the world and see if it was ready for me.

'OK. OK. I'm coming,' I grunted at my dad, flopping out of bed.

Twenty minutes later I had showered and dressed and was walking down to the bus stop, stuffing a piece of toast into my mouth. My skirt was twisted round the wrong way and my jumper felt like it was trying to strangle me. I reached the bus stop and threw my bag down, sighing. Another stinky Monday morning.

Dean and Jit walked up as I was wiping breadcrumbs from my mouth. They lived on the route of another bus but always walked to my stop each morning. God knows why – I've haven't even got the energy to get out of bed most mornings and those two walk for fifteen minutes just to catch the wrong bus. Boys . . .

'Late as usual,' said Jit and grinned.

'Fashionably,' I told him, noticing that his hair looked like it had been cut by a blind man with the shakes.

'Did little *Jitty-kins* lose his comb?' I asked in my worst 'stupid-girly' voice. 'Or is that your attempt at boy-band fashion?'

Dean laughed at Jit.

'Man, school ain't even *started* yet and you is getting dissed already . . .'

'*Wha*'? And I suppose that jumper is a fashion statement?' Jit replied, grinning at me.

I looked at my jumper, pretending that it looked fine to me.

'What's wrong with it, stupid boy . . . ?'

'You might wanna take it off and try again, Grace . . .' said Dean.

'Oh get stuffed, you little—' I began, only to be cut off by a couple of squealing boys wearing full uniform.

'*She's got her jumper on inside out . . .*'

I looked at my clothes again. They were right. In my rush to get down to the stop before I missed the bus I had forgotten to turn my jumper the right way round. I grinned at Jit and Dean to hide my embarrassment.

'S'meant to be inside out,' I told them, foolishly.

'Yeah, *right*,' laughed Jit.

I gave him a stare. I didn't care how good looking he was, he wasn't getting away with laughing at my appearance. *Boy* . . .

'It's a new design,' I said, styling it out, as Dean would have said.

'Don't even come with that, Grace,' said Dean, unimpressed. 'Just take it off and turn it the right way round . . .'

My name is Grace because I was born on a Monday and my grandmother was called Nina – which is Russian for Grace – or so my mum tells me. I'm twelve years old but don't let that fool you. I'm like a mini-adult according to my dad, the product of a generation 'ruined by television and mobile telephones . . .' My mum and dad are both thirty-eight and they always bang on about how in 'their day' the youth were more rebellious, always protesting and stuff. They sound like hippies, the ones from the Seventies, only my parents were like six when the hippie thing was big.

'Well, we were *born* in the Sixties,' my dad tells me, whenever I point out his age.

'You're just wannabes . . .' I usually reply.

'Cheeky little . . .'

'Stinky old man.'

My dad works as an architect with his best friend, Tommy. He works from home and is always 'just about to start work', normally with a cup of coffee in his hands. My mum is a social worker and spends a lot more time out of the house than my dad. She comes home stressed-out most evenings and she's the bad cop to my dad's good cop. If I ever want something that I'm not supposed to have, like a new top or a pair of trainers, I ask my dad because he's always got some new design on his mind, and says yes to almost anything, only to get told off by my mum when she gets home. I get my dad into a lot of trouble but he doesn't mind. I think he enjoys it.

Our house is in a nice area, according to most of my friends, and they usually spend quite a lot of time in the cellar which is huge. It's got a pool table in there, and sofas and a telly, so we use it as a hangout, which is lovely, apart from when my dad walks in and starts trying to act like he's 'in with the youngsters' by talking in rhyme like a rapper or '*cuffing*' the boys and telling them to '*cool out, man*'. That's when I wish I had a normal dad, instead of the weirdo that I do have, with his Jesus sandals and Bob Dylan T-shirts and shiny cords. I do love him to bits though, *groovy* beads and all.

I've got five really good friends from school. There's Dean who's thirteen and thinks he's an MC – he's even got a stupid name, MC D-C. His mum works with mine and his dad is cool. He owns a bar in town and he has the nicest smile.

Imtiaz is thirteen too. He's really tall and good looking, and one of those boys who's good at everything, from football to metalwork. All the girls like him – he's like the most popular boy in school. I don't fancy him though – he's not my type. He's uptight and always trying to act older than he is. His favourite phrase is 'grow up, we're not kids any more' which he mostly uses when he's talking to me or Dean. Or Jit.

Jit is the same age as Dean and Imtiaz. His mum is single – she works in a supermarket, and there's loads of stuff going on between Jit, his mum and the rest of his family, I think. I'm not too sure because Jit never really talks about his home life. He clams up when anyone talks about families and stuff. He's always getting into trouble with the teachers and the older lads at school.

Usually he gets Dean into trouble too. Jit's really clever but he hides it and he picks on me all the time. In a nice way though. We have a love/hate vibe, according to my dad, who gets on really well with him. Hannah thinks Jit fancies me cos he's always round our house, even when the others aren't there. My mum jokes that he should move in but my stinky older brother, Charlie, is enough, with his smelly room and his grey socks that used to be white. I couldn't handle living in the same house as two teenage boys. I'd rather slap myself in the face with a wet fish.

The girls are called Suky and Hannah and they're both thirteen too. Suky is really tall and skinny and athletic. She's like the girl version of Imtiaz. She's the leader whenever we argue or have to discuss things and she's always beating the boys in races and other sporty stuff. She even beat Imtiaz in 'keep ups' with a football, which really wound him up for a while. Not too long though. He and Suky are really close and I think they would make a good couple. Suky wants to be an actress when she's older.

Hannah's a good laugh. She's really clever and sometimes she's a bit fiery but mostly she's really cool. Her mum works in the same supermarket as Jit's mum. Jit and Hannah grew up together, going to the same school since they were five, along with Dean. Suky,

Imtiaz and me went to the same schools too, so when we got to our current school we were like two little gangs joining up into one. Hannah wants to be a journalist and is desperate to set up a school newspaper, only our principal, Mr Black, claims there isn't enough time or money to do one.

That's our gang then. I suppose I should get back to the story, really . . .

TWO

The bus took twenty-five minutes to get through the traffic before it reached the school and by that time it was full of kids shouting and screaming and throwing things out of the window. Like a zoo but on wheels, with an upper and lower deck. I got up slowly and followed the boys, catching my foot against a giant black sports bag that had been left, thoughtfully, in the aisle. I swore and heard a deep, 'I'm nearly a man' laugh. It was the bag's owner, an older boy, Jason Patel.

'Wanna watch where you're goin' sexy . . .' he said to me with a smirk.

'Get stuffed . . .'

'*Easy* – gal thinks she's funny, innit . . .' he said to his mates, who all joined him in laughing at me.

'I'm sorry?' I asked, pretending that I didn't understand what he meant.

'*I'm sorry* . . .' he mimicked.

'Come on Grace,' said Jit, from the stairwell.

'Better go join yer boyfriend, sexy . . .' smiled Jason.

'And *you'd* better get to the dentist. Yellow teeth . . . Big no-no.'

I walked away quickly as Jason's face turned red with anger and his mates started laughing, telling him to clean his teeth. He called me a rude name as I went downstairs and got off the bus. Jit and Dean were standing in the bus shelter waiting for me.

'Let's try and get to school on time for once, man,' said Jit, as the bus cleared of passengers.

The stop was about a quarter of a mile from the school gates and we walked slowly down the road, other kids running past us to get in before the registration bell went. Jason and his mates ran past too, calling me names. Jit called Jason a few back. But then Jason stopped and turned round.

'You what?' he shouted.

'You're in the dog-do now, man,' grinned Dean.

Jit looked like he was about to apologise but instead he shrugged and carried on walking. Jason shouted something about 'another time' and ran off after his friends, his bag bouncing on his back.

'Dickhead . . .' spat Jit.

'Don't worry about it,' replied Dean. 'If the man is so bad he would have dealt it right there . . .'

'I ain't scared of him . . .' said Jit.

'God – you two are *soooo* tough,' I laughed, trying to wind them up.

'Shut up and wipe the crumbs off your face,' said Jit, smiling.

'*Stinky bas—*'

I didn't have time to finish because the bell sounded and we were only just at the gates. Ahead of us, Mr Black was standing at the main entrance, looking at his watch and shaking his head. As we walked up he tut-tutted.

'And good evening to you three,' he said, straightening his tie knot.

'Bus was late . . .' mumbled Jit, not looking at him.

'I believe that if you had caught an earlier bus—' began Black but Dean cut him off. Big mistake.

'There was traffic, man.'

'Now, now, Dean. We don't interrupt people when they are speaking, do we?'

'Nossir.'

'Because that would be very rude of us, now wouldn't it . . . ?'

'Yessir.'

'Right then. Now get to your form rooms and if I see you dawdle into school tomorrow I'll have to give you detention . . .'

'*But sir—*' I began, only to be interrupted by the

man who had just told Dean it was wrong to do just that.

'Firm but fair, young lady. Firm but fair . . .'

'Unlike your belly,' whispered Jit as Mr Black walked out of earshot.

'Unlike *which* one – the firm or the fair?' I asked him.

'Definitely the *firm* man. Black need some serious exercise . . .'

'You'll be like that one day.' I said with a grin.

'Maybe so,' replied Jit, 'but I won't be walking round with toast stuck to me face like you, will I?'

'*Dissed* . . .' laughed Dean, giving me a bear hug.

'Gerroff . . . !'

Mrs Dooher, our form tutor, was reading out names as we joined our class mates. As usual, I went and sat down with Suky and Hannah, at a table just in front of the boys. Imtiaz shook his head and laughed as we walked in.

'One of these days you lot will be on time,' he said, like he was our dad or something.

'Just cos you like to get here before the caretaker don't mean we have to,' replied Jit, winking at me.

I couldn't wink back because every time I try, both my eyelids close and I look like I'm constipated, so I just smiled back and said nothing. Mrs Dooher looked up from her register and smiled. She was my favourite teacher, a bit like a surrogate mother, with her soft Liverpool accent and stories of being asked out by some old bloke called Paul McCartney who used to be in a band called the Beatles. I had to raid my dad's record collection to find out who he was. A pop star but a real one with talent – not like the rubbish that fills the charts nowadays, according to my dad. Mrs Dooher gave us the dreaded announcement – late lunch week. Again. Then she stood up and shuffled over to where we were sitting.

'I'm going to have to tell you off for being late again,' she said with a smile.

'We're sorry,' I told her, answering for Jit and Dean too.

'You're always sorry, Grace. I can't keep making excuses for you all . . .'

'Won't happen again, Miss,' Dean replied. 'Honest.'

'I dunno,' she said, smiling again.

Dean grinned and then got up and gave her a hug.

'You're *lurrvely* . . .' he told her, in a silly accent.

'You cheeky *get* . . .' she replied.

'Do we have to be on late lunches again, Miss?' he asked her.

The others didn't hear him. They were busy gossiping about school stuff. But I wanted to know what he was talking about.

'It's on the rota, Dean. That's the way it goes . . .'

'But *Miss* – the food's always cold and that . . .'

'And *what* . . . ?'

'I'm sorry?'

Mrs Dooher smiled again. 'You say "*and that*" after every sentence. I was just wondering "*and what*" exactly,' she asked.

'It's just street banter, you get me?' replied Dean.

'Do I?' grinned Mrs Dooher.

'What?' asked Dean, confused.

'*Get you*. Do I *really* get you . . . ?'

'Oh you're just takin' the piss . . .'

'*Dean* . . .' replied Mrs Dooher, pretending to be stern.

'The mickey, I mean.'

'That's better.' she said. 'Now get off to your lessons and leave me to prepare for the nightmare that is Year 10 Home Economics.'

The others were already on their way to lessons as I pulled Dean to one side and asked him why he was bothered by being on late lunch all of a sudden.

'The food's nasty,' he told me. 'All cold and that . . .'

'And *what*?' I replied, a feeble attempt to continue a bad joke, I know.

'Grace . . .'

'But we've had a lunch rota since we got here,' I said.

'Yeah – I know that but it don't mean we have to like it. You remember that silly rhyme – *School Dinners*?'

'Yeah. "*Concrete chips, concrete chips. Sloppy semolina . . .*"'

'Relax, man. Ain't no need to make it rain by singing the thing . . .'

I stopped singing and pouted at him but he just ignored me.

'Well I reckon we should complain . . .' he said.

'Who to, Dean? No one is going to change the rules because of us . . .'

'Don't mean we shouldn't complain,' he moaned, as we walked after the rest of our form group.

I sang the silly rhyme all the way to French, in a French accent, until Dean put me in a headlock to make me stop – stinky boy.

THREE

We were standing in the dinner queue later on when Dean started going on about cold food again.

'See what I mean? Everyone else has had their food but we've got to wait till last and then all we get to eat is cold chips.'

'Speak for yourself,' I told him. 'I don't eat chips.'

'Well what are you gonna eat today then?'

I waited a few moments until we'd reached the service hatch and looked at what was on offer. Dean's concrete chips were there, looking the worse for wear, together with something that looked as though it might be lasagne. There were about two fish cakes in a separate steel tray, some burnt sausages and what seemed to be pizza portions too. I couldn't tell because the topping was black and crispy. Beside these tempting dishes sat a tray of Cellophane-wrapped sandwiches with hand-written stickers telling us what they had in them. Egg mayonnaise, tuna salad, cheese salad, ham salad. Even *salad* salad for the vegans. The bread looked like it had been stepped on by an elephant and the plastic was all sweaty. I turned my nose up and picked up a bruised banana, two apples and a bottle of water.

'I'm on a diet,' I told Dean.

'See? The food is *rank*,' he replied, looking at his wedge of looky-likey lasagne and brittle potato.

'Oh shut up and quit complaining, you girl!'

'Well, would *you* eat this?'

I turned up my nose again. 'No – I'm on a diet.'

We walked over to the table where the rest of our friends were sitting. Imtiaz and Suky were whispering something to each other and Hannah was telling Jit about how much the school needed its own paper. Jit looked bored as he tried to spear his chips with a fork. One of the chips flew off the plate and landed on the table making Jit and Hannah laugh.

'Are you two ever gonna grow up?' asked Imtiaz, looking disgusted.

'*Are you two ever gonna grow up*!' mimicked Jit, grinning.

'See what I mean?' continued Imtiaz, looking at Suky.

As Dean and I sat down, Jit picked up the offending chip and threw it at Imtiaz's head. It bounced off his temple and landed in the plate of one of our form group, Mohammed.

'Oi . . . !'

'Easy Mohammed,' laughed Jit. 'No need to get your panties in a . . .'

'KOONER!!!!!'

Jit groaned. The shout had come from Mr Herbert, enemy No. 1 and all round grump.

'Food is for eating,' Mr Herbert bellowed across three tables, spitting everywhere.

'Yessir,' mumbled Jit.

'Don't you "yessir" me, young man. World full of starving people and here you are throwing precious food around . . .'

'Man, ain't like I can post it to 'em, is it?' said Jit, making everyone under the age of sixteen snigger.

'Looks like the shit was posted to *us*,' added Dean, just loud enough to be heard.

Herbert's face began to redden. 'MY OFFICE!'

I looked at Jit and shook my head. Jit shrugged his shoulders and stood up.

'Can't even finish me dinner . . .' he said. 'What is this – *prison* . . . ?'

'You too, Dean Chambers,' continued Herbert.

'Ah sir!' moaned Dean, throwing his fork down on his plate.

'Don't "Ah sir" me. As if I haven't a million and one things to do with my lunchtime already . . .'

Dean swore under his breath, stood up and slammed

his chair under the table, sending my water spilling. I moved my legs out of its path as it poured off the table but I didn't say anything to Dean. He was angry enough as it was.

Then I did something really stupid.

'You know, Mr Herbert, lunch is a basic human right,' I said, really smarmy.

Herbert looked at me like he was in shock. I think he expected lip from Jit and Dean but from a nice middle class girl like me? I sat and waited for him to respond, hoping that he would close his mouth so that I didn't have to look at his manky teeth.

'I'm sorry, young lady, I seem to have missed what you said?' he replied, daring me to say it again.

'Well it's true,' I continued. 'We have to be here at half eight in the morning through until well after three in the afternoon, which is a long time. Therefore, lunch is a basic human right . . .' I paused for effect, realising that I was going to be joining Jit and Dean in Herbert's office. '. . . And you're denying that right to my friends.'

'Well perhaps you'd like to complain to the European Court, Grace Parkhurst. Until then you can join your fellow idiots in my office. *MOVE*!'

I stood up and grinned at Jit before answering.

'There's no need to be so rude, is there?' I said, following the lads out of the dinner hall.

* * *

We had History straight after lunch, but by the time Herbert had finished with us we were late. I made all the excuses to Mr Woods, our teacher, who just ushered us in and told us to sit down. We were studying Britain's Roman history and halfway through the lesson Dean leaned over and whispered to me.

'There's a way out of having to eat late lunches,' he said.

'I'm *trying* to listen,' I told him, hoping that Mr Woods wouldn't see us talking. Getting into trouble once in a week was enough for me, never mind twice in one day.

'There's these things called socials,' continued Dean.

Jit, who was sitting on my other side, asked me what Dean was saying.

I elbowed Dean and told Jit to be quiet, as Mr Woods talked about something called the Fosse Way.

'What's he on about?' whispered Jit, a little too loudly.

'The Fosse Way, Jit,' said Mr Woods. 'Perhaps you have something to share?'

'Nossir,' replied Jit, pinching me on my thigh under the table.

'OWW!' I cried. Well, it hurt.

'Grace – what is going on?' asked Mr Woods.

'Nothing, sir. I got cramp . . .'

'Well stop it and pay attention . . .'

I gave Jit a death glare and returned to listening to Woods.

Dean kept quiet for maybe five minutes before he leaned over again.

'There's these socials . . .' he picked up where he'd left off.

'Shut up!' I whispered back.

'But . . .'

'Write it down,' I hissed, making a note of something that Mr Woods had just said.

Dean scribbled something in his pad and ripped it out quietly, folding it and passing it over. I waited until Mr Woods walked over to the windows as he spoke before opening it under the desk. I made out the words '*social*' and '*early lunch*'. I put the note on my writing pad and wrote '*what are you banging on about*?' underneath Dean's message, folded it and gave it back.

Jit leaned across me to see what was going on.

'Will you three please pay attention . . .' said Mr Woods, raising his voice, something that he rarely did.

'Sorry sir,' I replied, going red in the face.

Woods carried on with his lecture as Dean read my reply. He started to write another message but I elbowed him again and shook my head. 'I'm not interested,' I whispered, ignoring him for the rest of the lesson. I couldn't work out his obsession with lunches. He was doing my head in.

Jit came back to my house after school and we sat in the cellar watching telly and drinking orange juice, freshly squeezed by my dad. Jit was moaning about the bits in it, telling me that it wasn't like the stuff that you got from Asda that came out of a carton.

'It's fresh,' I told him, not wanting to push it because my parents could afford to buy fresh food everyday and Jit's mum couldn't.   J206,008

'But the bits get stuck in your teeth . . .'

'I can get you some dental floss if you like. Or a toothpick . . .'

Jit put his glass down and got up, walking over to the pool table. He started racking the balls.

'What were you and Dean talking about in History?' he asked, looking for the cue.

'Nothing really.'

'Didn't look like nothing,' he said, breaking off. 'You playin'?'

'With Dean?' I said, smiling. I knew that he was talking about pool but I just couldn't resist the wind-up.

Jit gave me a weird look as I got up and joined him at the table.

'He was trying to tell me about some theory he's got – how to get out of late lunches. I dunno what's got into him . . .' I said.

'He gets a bit funny sometimes,' replied Jit, before missing an easy shot.

I grabbed the cue and shoved Jit out of the way with my hip.

'You're rubbish . . . Here let me show you how to play.'

I potted three balls before it was Jit's turn again.

'Yeah well, I'd be like king of pool if I had one of these in my house . . .' he said, missing again.

'See? Rubbish!'

'So do you like . . . fancy him?' asked Jit, casually, not looking at me as he gave me the cue.

'Who?' I asked vaguely, playing dumb.

'Dean . . .'

'No. He's not my type . . .'

Jit looked puzzled.

'Why?' he asked me.

'Because he's a stinky boy – that's why . . .'

'Don't you like boys?'

'Yeah – just not Dean. Not like that anyway . . .'

'So who *do* you like?' he said, going a bit red.

'Dunno,' I replied, honestly. 'I've never really thought about it, Jit.'

'Oh . . .'

There was a knock at the door and then Hannah appeared at the foot of the stairs.

'Hey!'

'Hi Han – wanna watch me beat Jit at pool?'

Hannah grinned and sat down, picking up my glass of juice without asking, and drinking from it.

'URRGH! This has got bits in it,' she said.

'I told her that,' said Jit, obviously happy not to continue our earlier conversation. Strange boy.

'It's fresh,' I repeated. 'It's supposed to be like that . . .'

'Oh shut up and take your shot, fancy pants,' grinned Hannah.

Stinky gimps . . .

FOUR

My mum got in from work around half past six and by that point Hannah and Jit had been invited to stay for dinner by my dad, who had appeared in the cellar doorway wearing beige cords, a green shirt open to the navel and sandals, with an apron wrapped around his middle. He told us that he was making vegetarian sausages with ratatouille. I thought Jit would turn his nose up at that but he was too busy smirking at my dad's embarrassing dress sense to actually hear what he was saying. By the time my mum had sat down at the table and made her regular joke about opening a soup kitchen for the waifs and strays that I seemed to bring home from school, Jit had no choice but to eat the food in front of him.

'How is it, Jit?' my dad asked him. ' "*Kickin*" or "*stink*," as you groovy cats say these days . . . ?'

'*Dad!*' I said, cringing.

'Relax Grace – just because I've a few more years than you doesn't mean—'

'I think you'll find it does, Michael,' interrupted my mum with an amused look on her face.

'I think you're quite cool, Mr Parkhurst,' said Hannah, managing to keep a straight face.

'Yeah, the food's . . . er . . . groovy man,' added Jit.

'Wonderful,' smiled my dad, beaming, completely ignorant of the fact that everyone was having a laugh at his expense.

My mum asked Hannah how school was going.

'It's OK, Mrs Parkhurst – they still won't let me do a school newspaper though.'

'You and your school paper – man, that's all you ever chat about . . .' said Jit, picking at the food with his fork.

'I'm sure it would be quite a good idea,' replied my mum before Hannah could swear at Jit.

'Yeah,' I added. 'We could write a gossip column and do news reports on everyone . . .'

'*And* voice *our* opinions about what the teachers make us do,' said Hannah. 'Like in a proper democracy . . .'

'What's that then, Professor Hannah, a new dance or something?' laughed Jit.

'Democracy is a system of government by the people within which—' began my dad, really seriously.

'I kinda know what it is, Mr Parkhurst,' admitted Jit, with a grin.

'I think you're becoming the butt of yet another joke,' my mum told Dad with a smile.

'I *knew* that . . .' he pretended.

He was good at pretending that he knew things. He had this theory that it was better to know a little bit about a lot than to know a lot about not very much. My mum called it the cow poo argument.

'Anyway,' continued Hannah, ignoring Jit, 'if the teachers and the governors and everyone gets to tell us what to do, then we should have a right to tell them what we think of it. I mean it's not like I'm saying they should let us have longer holidays or half the day off . . .'

'It's a very valid point,' agreed my mum. 'What do you think Grace?'

'Well I suppose it would be good and I do think we should be allowed to tell the teachers what we think.'

'I'm very surprised at Mr Black,' said my mum. 'You would think that he might jump at something else to shout about on local radio . . .'

'I was on the Internet the other day,' added Hannah, 'and in Birmingham they've got this Young People's Parliament thing . . . and we can't even get a paper going.'

Jit groaned.

'Do we have to talk about the stupid newspaper . . .'

'Why – was there something else you wanted to talk about?' asked my dad.

'Nah – it's just that in my house we just eat and watch the telly and that. I ain't used to all this *deep* conversation bit . . .'

My mum looked at me and then at Hannah.

'Is your mum on the same shift as Hannah's mum again,' she asked Jit.

'Er . . . yeah,' he said, really quickly. 'I've finished . . . can I go back down into the cellar . . . ?'

'Of course you can,' Mum said, and smiled.

'Thank you for dinner, Mr Parkhurst,' mumbled Jit, looking embarrassed, before he bolted out of his chair and down the stairs to the cellar.

I waited until he'd gone before speaking.

'He's a bit shy sometimes . . .' I said.

'He'll talk when he's ready,' replied my mum, the voice of experience. 'Boys are different to girls at this age . . .'

'He's just a weirdo,' grinned Hannah. 'Been like that since he was five . . .'

Everyone laughed, lightening the mood a bit and then Mum started to clear up the plates.

'Grace, could you load these things into the dishwasher for me,' she said.

'OK. And then can I take my bike and walk Hannah and Jit home? I'll ride straight back . . .'

'Fine, but take my mobile with you just in case.'

We walked back about half an hour later. Well, I *wobbled* along on my bike and the other two walked. The route took us past a row of shops and through an alleyway where two lads had written some pointless graffiti on the fence: '*Bali and Parmy – Safe!*' – nothing else. No artwork or clever stuff. Just that. Silly people. At the end of the alley we turned into a long road and I asked Jit why he didn't like talking about stuff at home. He gave me a funny look, shrugged, and then changed the subject.

'Your dad's funny, man,' he said, smiling. 'I don't mean funny bad – funny as in good. He makes me laugh and that . . .'

'Yeah, he's embarrassing,' I replied.

Hannah gave Jit a look.

'You're weird, Jit,' she told him.

'I ain't . . .'

'Yeah you are. Grace asked you a question about you and you turned it round and started talking about her dad – if that isn't weird I dunno what is,' she continued.

'I ain't got nothing to say – that's all . . .' he replied, looking sheepish.

'You know that you can talk to us if there's something wrong,' I added.

Jit glared at me.

'*What makes you think* . . . ? Never mind. Forget it. I just don't talk like you girls do . . .'

'But you could. If you wanted to . . .' I said again.

'Only I don't, so let's just leave it at that, man . . .' he replied, looking away.

'You're a weirdo . . .' said Hannah, smiling.

'Yeah, yeah,' said Jit, dismissively, as we rounded another corner and walked up to the cross-roads where I was going to turn back.

Something shot past us, over the tops of our heads. A stone. It bounced off the roof of a car in front of us.

'What the . . . ?'

'Let's see how tough you are now, man!' came a shout from behind us.

We turned together to see Jason Patel and two of his friends behind us. Jit tensed up immediately and clenched his fists. I looked at Hannah who just shrugged. Then another stone flew right past her head and she went mad, shouting at Jason and his mates.

'Who you throwin' stones at, you arseholes?'

They rode up to us on their bikes and started to circle us. Jason kicked out at Jit as he passed him and then they started laughing. Jit was going red in the face and

I started to get scared. Hannah stood where she was, her eyes blazing.

'Oh *yeah* – you're bad boys, you are,' she told them.

'Badder than you . . .' said Jason, kicking out at Jit again.

'*Get lost!*' shouted Jit, watching Jason as he came round again.

'See how you got your girlfriends to back you up . . .' Jason said to Jit, laughing.

He went to kick at Jit again, only this time Jit grabbed his leg and yanked him off his bike. Jason went flying, ending up in a tangle with the frame. The other two lads got off their bikes and grabbed Jit, shoving him around. And then I heard a car horn beeping. The car pulled to a stop and Mr Singh, a sports teacher at school, jumped out, still wearing his tracksuit. '*What the hell do you think you're doing* . . . ?' he shouted at Jason and his mates.

The two lads that had hold of Jit let him go, grabbed their bikes and rode off. Jason tried to follow them but Mr Singh grabbed hold of him.

'*Gerroff me!*' shouted Jason.

'What do you think you're doing?' demanded Mr Singh.

'I'll tell my dad . . .' squealed Jason. 'He'll get the police onto you . . .'

Mr Singh let go of Jason and shrugged.

'Call them right now,' he told Jason, holding out his own mobile.

'Tosser . . .' said Jason, grabbing his bike.

'Ain't so tough now . . .' Hannah said, laughing.

Jason glared at Jit.

'See *you* tomorrow,' he said with a sneer, before riding off after his mates.

Mr Singh asked us if we were OK before telling Jit and Hannah that he would drive them home. Jit tried to put on a bad boy act and said that he'd be fine, but Mr Singh insisted and Jit eventually agreed.

'How about you, Grace?' Mr Singh asked me.

'I'll be OK. I've got my bike and I only live round the corner,' I said, feeling a little less scared.

'OK then, but go straight home and if you get any more trouble from that lot – you tell me,' he said, talking to all of us.

'See you in the morning,' said Hannah.

'Yeah,' I replied, looking at Jit. 'You OK Jit?'

'Yeah . . . see you later, Grace.'

I got on my bike and rode home, wondering whether Jason would have a go at Jit in school the next day. When I got in, my mum saw that my face was red and asked me if I was all right.

'Yeah,' I told her. 'Just rode back too quickly . . .'

FIVE

Mr Black was waiting at the school gates the next morning, as usual, but he seemed to be in such a good mood that he forgot to tell us off as we walked in late. He said something about the birds singing and it being a beautiful day and ushered us into the school.

As we walked down to our form room I wondered whether to bring up what had happened with Jason the evening before. But Jit was busy teasing Dean about a spot on his nose.

'Must be hard having that thing stuck to the end of your nose – must interfere with your sight,' he said, as Dean told him to get lost for about the fiftieth time.

'Ah – don't be arsey about it – we've all had 'em,' teased Jit. 'Ain't that right, Grace?'

'What?' I asked as we walked into our form room and Mrs Dooher looked up from her desk, shaking her head at us.

'*Spots*,' replied Jit, lowering his voice. 'We've all had spots . . .'

'Stop winding Dean up, Jit,' I told him, taking a seat

next to Hannah, who was doodling on a notepad. Jit ignored me.

'Thing's got a life of its own. Man, it's so big it's probably got its own atmosphere . . .' he continued.

Dean kissed his teeth at Jit and turned his back on him.

'Like a planet sitting on the end of your conk – you're own likkle planet . . .'

'And you can talk 'bout conks?' Hannah told Jit, winking at me.

'What?' asked Jit, screwing up his face.

'Man, if I had a nose the size of yours I wouldn't be laughing at no one else . . .'

Jit went red and shut up.

'See dat man! You soon hush up when *you* get dissed . . .' laughed Dean, ruffling Jit's hair.

'Gerroff you dutty!'

'Calm down now form,' interrupted Mrs Dooher, standing up and facing us all. '*Calm down*! *Calm down*!' mimicked a lad called Raj from behind us, pretending to be a scouser. Mrs Dooher gave him a look that told him what an idiot he was before she continued.

'Excuse the comedian at the back, form. Right, some of you may have noticed that our esteemed principal, Mr Black, is in a good mood this morning . . .'

'Man acted like he was off his head on something when we come in . . .' replied Jit.

'. . . *Came* in, Jit. You *came* in . . .' corrected Mrs Dooher.

'Whatever . . .'

'Well there's a good reason for Mr Black's mood. The school has just been given funding to rebuild the library and turn the old, disused block into a media and languages centre . . .'

The disused block was round the back of the school and had been empty for years. Some of the pupils said it was haunted, but according to my dad it was just an old Victorian building that was going to ruin. At my first ever parents' evening at the school he had proceeded to tell Mr Black what a shame that was, before offering to buy it and do it up. Strange man.

The rest of the form '*oohed*' and '*ahhed*' at the mention of new funding and Mrs Dooher went on to explain that the work was going to start in the next few months, meaning that the new building would be ready by the following school year. Pushpa, one of the girls, gave everyone a letter for their parents, outlining the plans. When she got to Jit, he blew her a kiss and she turned bright red, running off to her seat, where her friends began to tease her.

'You flirt,' I said to him.

'You jealous . . . ?' he asked me, smiling.

'You wish, stinky boy . . .'

It was meant as a joke but Jit gave me a funny look before pouting and turning his attention back to Dean's zit. This time Suky and Imtiaz told Jit to stop.

'Man, all you lot is boring . . .' said Suky.

'Act your age for a change, Jit,' added Imtiaz.

'Like you act yours you mean? *Sixty* . . . ?'

'Will you little beggars shut up!' shouted Mrs Dooher. Well actually, it was more like she raised her voice because she was far too lovely to shout. And even in raising her voice she broke into a smile.

'You're rubbish at tellin' us off, Miss,' laughed Dean.

'Ooh you cheeky little . . .'

'Just tell him to take his zit and get lost!' shouted Jit.

'Why don't you—?' began Dean.

'All right, all right lads . . .' said Mrs Dooher calming them down. 'Off you all go to your lessons and don't forget that the music room is being painted and is out of bounds for a few days . . .'

The rest of what she said got lost in the din as the form scraped back their chairs and went off to lessons. I followed Hannah out of the classroom, with Imi and Suky. Behind us, Mrs Dooher called out to Dean and as he went to speak to her she handed him a note. He opened it, read it and then stuffed it into one of his trouser pockets, grinning to himself.

I'm often told that I'm too nosy, always wanting to

know what's going on, so I tried really hard not to wonder about what had been in the note. It didn't work though. By the time we got to Science, I would have given him my lunch money to find out what it said. Only he wouldn't say, telling me to shut up and pay attention. And when I tried to get Jit to join in with my nosing all I got from him was a funny look and a shrug. Boys . . .

At break time we stood around by the tennis courts to one side of the main school building. The courts were full of boys playing football and running around yelling at each other. Groups of girls stood and watched them, staring at the ones that they fancied. Hannah was talking about an article that she'd read in a newspaper about exactly which bugs hid in which type of meat. She was telling us about how dirty chickens were and how they had some kind of organism living in their bottoms when Jit swore. I stopped listening to Hannah and gave Jit a funny look.

'Jason Patel,' he said, nodding towards the lower tennis court.

'Raas!' said Dean, whatever that meant.

Jason and two of his goons were walking over, all scary looking.

Instinctively I looked around for a teacher. There were

two of them, Mr Singh, and a young English teacher called Miss Khan, standing by the entrance to the school, holding mugs of coffee. If I hadn't been so preoccupied with Jason I would have pointed out to Hannah that Mr Singh and Miss Khan seemed to be flirting with each other, only I was scared, so I told Hannah that I was going to tell them about Jason. She nodded and told me that she'd wait with Jit and Dean. I was walking over to Mr Singh when I heard the shouting start.

'*FIGHT! FIGHT! FIGHT!*'

Groups of people gathered around as Jason swore at Jit and Dean, calling them 'grasses'. Hannah tried to intervene but one of Jason's mates shoved her to one side and then Jason and Jit started to have a scrap. Lots of the younger lads started egging them on and then I heard a whistle. It was Mr Singh, who was sprinting over to the commotion. Behind him, three more male teachers came running out of school. I turned back to the fight and saw Dean punch one of Jason's friends. Jit was on the floor with Jason kneeling on his chest, punching him in the face.

Mr Singh grabbed Jason and held him whilst the other teachers took hold of Dean, Jit and Jason's friends, who were all swearing at each other. Yet more teachers ran out and told the rest of the pupils to get inside to lessons. I started to walk into school with Hannah when Mr Singh called us back.

'You two were there yesterday so I'd like you to stay and help sort this mess out,' he said, letting Mr Woods and the other teachers take Jason and his mates to Mr Black's office.

'But I don't know why . . .' I began.

'I still need to talk to you, Grace,' said Mr Singh.

Dean and Jit were standing next to him. Jit had a swollen eye, which he kept on touching. He looked really angry.

'*Well*?' asked Mr Singh as Hannah and me joined the lads.

'Well what?' replied Dean, angrily.

'Yesterday I had to stop a fight between Jit and Jason and now, today, I've had to do the same thing. What's going on . . . ?'

'Ask dem man,' said Dean. 'It's my boy standing here with a bust-up eye . . .'

'I'm asking *you*, Dean,' Mr Singh told him.

'Jason just picked on them,' said Hannah. 'It's not their fault that he's a bully . . .'

'Is that what it is, Jit? Jason's bullying you . . . ?'

Jit gave Hannah a death stare and then shrugged.

'It's nuttin' man,' he told Mr Singh.

'It's obviously more than nothing, son. I know that

you didn't start it. But I need you to report Jason. That way Mr Black can take some kind of action . . .'

'Sack that – me nah grass up no-one . . .' said Jit, defiantly.

⋆'An' nuh bother even ask *me* . . .' added Dean.

Hannah shook her head at them.

'It's not grassin',' she said.

'Yeah – it's not . . .' I agreed, only for Jit and Dean to shoot me a look each. Looks that said shut up.

'We need to do something. This isn't the first time – Jason's already on a warning . . .' said Mr Singh.

'It's nothin',' repeated Jit, sullenly.

'Look – you two are no good to the football team if you've been beaten up,' said Mr Singh, trying a different tack, but the lads just ignored him, and looked at the floor.

'Fine . . . but this will get out of hand unless something is done . . .' said Mr Singh. 'Now, get to your next lesson and remember, if anything like this happens again, tell me.'

Hannah led the way back into school, her eyes blazing with anger at Jit and Dean.

'You two are so messed up . . .'

'What do you know about it?' asked Jit, touching his eye again.

'You gonna let Jason get away with it? He's a bully . . .'

'We'll deal with him our way,' replied Dean.

'Yeah – because you're so *bad* . . .' sneered Hannah.

Jit ignored her and asked me what the next lesson was.

'Maths,' I said, smiling at him, hoping that he would calm down.

'Sack that – I'm not going . . .' he said, walking off in the other direction.

'*Jit!*' I called out after him.

'Leave him, Grace,' said Hannah. 'He'll be OK in a while . . .'

'But he'll get into trouble . . .' I said, really concerned.

'Trouble follows him around,' said Dean. 'He's used to it.'

We walked into our classroom and sat down. Mrs Lee-Cross, the Maths teacher, asked us why we were late.

'They was fightin', Miss!' someone shouted out.

'And where's Jit?' she asked us.

As Dean and Hannah shrugged and sat down, I waited for one of them to say something. When they didn't, I did.

'He's got a black eye, Miss. I think he's with Mr Singh . . .'

'Oh – thank you, Grace. Now let's get down to mathematics . . .'

SIX

The lesson was boring but then again I always thought Maths lessons were that way. It was one of those things that I just couldn't find any enthusiasm for, no matter how hard I tried. My dad had taken to giving me extra tuition at home, only his tuition was about as useful as an eighty-year-old in a boy band. We were constantly interrupted by phone calls from his clients, too. Not that I ever complained. It was lovely of him to try in the first place. In the end my mum twigged on that I wasn't doing as well as I could and she got me Maths tutor software for my computer. It's still in the box, wrapped in its Cellophane, gathering dust in the no-go zone under my bed. With all the other fun things that you can do with a PC, like chatting to people on the Net and instant messaging, why would I want to use it to learn boring, stinky maths?

But it wasn't just the lesson, I was worried about Jit too, wondering where he had gone. Mr Black stalked the corridors of Devana High like a security guard during lessons, on the look out for skiving pupils and 'unwanted visitors' as he liked to call them. A year before we had got to the school, there had been an incident in which a pervy bloke had walked into the school and locked himself in the girls' toilets. It was in the papers and on the local TV news, and the school had tightened security because of it. Hence Mr Black's walkabouts.

I was busy thinking of good places to hide in if you were going to skive a lesson, when Mrs Lee-Cross told some of the pupils that they could go. I looked at my watch. It was ten to twelve. Four lads got up, all from the same table and walked to the door. And then Dean scraped back his chair and joined them. I looked up at him, wondering where he was going.

Imtiaz nudged me.

'Where's he off to?' he whispered.

'Dunno,' I replied.

'He's trying it on, I reckon,' said Suky, leaning across the table.

Mrs Lee-Cross gave Dean a raised eyebrow and then continued to talk about some maths problem or other, as I sat with my mouth open and watched him walk out with the gang of nerds.

'Well, he got away with it,' whispered Imtiaz.

'Maybe he's gone to find Jit,' added Hannah.

'Yeah, that'll be it,' I agreed.

'Are you three listening to *me* or having your own

conversation?' asked Mrs Lee-Cross over the heads of the other pupils.

'Listening to you, Miss,' replied Imtiaz. 'Honest . . .'

'Good, then perhaps one of your table would care to work out the problem I've just been outlining . . . Grace, why don't you tell us the solution . . .'

I sat there, conscious that my face was turning redder by the second. I could hear Imtiaz sniggering as I '*ummed*' and '*aahed*'.

'Er . . . well Miss . . .' I began, wishing that I'd paid attention.

I didn't see Dean all lunchtime and Jit only surfaced about ten minutes before we were due at afternoon registration, with a purple bruise around his eye and a face like thunder. The rest of us were finishing up our lunches in the dining hall, discussing ways to convince Mr Black that we needed a school newspaper. Imtiaz saw Jit coming first.

'Here's a story for it . . . "*Boy Gets Given Black Eye*" . . .' he said, as we turned to Jit.

'You OK?' asked Suky, getting up and putting her arm around him.

'Do I look like I'm OK?' snapped Jit.

Suky pulled back from him, hurt, and his face softened a bit.

'Sorry,' he said, surprising all of us. It was a word that he didn't use very often.

'It's no problem, Jit,' smiled Suky, with a sisterly concern in her eyes.

'You should have told Singhy what happened,' said Imtiaz.

'Yeah – but then Jason would have got into even more trouble . . .'

'*So*? That's his problem . . .' replied Imtiaz.

'And mine the next time I see him out on the street – 's'all right for you . . . he lives near me . . .'

'Yeah but he ain't that tough . . .' said Imtiaz. 'And anyway, if he touches you outside school you can have him done for assault or something . . .'

Jit shook his head and looked at Hannah. 'Don't work that way, bro',' he said. 'It always come back to you. If it ain't him, it's his mates . . .'

'Man, you make it sound like you live in the Bronx or somewhere like that. It's not that bad . . .'

'Yeah but it's a different place to where you live, Imi,' added Hannah, in support of Jit.

'Whatever . . .' replied Imtiaz.

I could feel an argument coming so I decided to do my usual and change the subject.

'Where do you think Dean's got to?' I asked.

Jit gave me another of his looks. 'What's up with

Dean?' he asked, looking a bit concerned, as though maybe Dean had got into more trouble with Jason Patel.

'He got out of Maths early – same time as the nerds – and Little Miss Won't-Mind-My-Own is wondering why . . .' said Hannah.

'Well – at least I'm honest,' I replied, defending myself. 'And anyway, if you're going to be a journalist *you'll* have to develop a nosy streak too . . .'

'I thought he'd gone looking for you, Jit,' said Suky, stabbing at her food with a fork.

'You don't have to kill that you know – thing dead already . . .' replied Jit, pointing at the mush on her plate.

'Just checking . . .' she replied, smiling.

Mr Black's voice bellowed around the hall, telling us to leave. '*Come along Devana High – it's time for the dinner staff to clear up now that you've had your lunches . . . It's only . . .*'

'Fair . . .' mimicked Suky.

We got up to leave, taking our trays to the counter. Hannah and Suky walked off ahead with Imtiaz, in a hurry to get to English, which they loved. I hung back with Jit.

'So Dean didn't try to find you . . . ?' I asked.

'Man, you seem really interested in Dean lately,' he

snapped. But then he looked like he regretted what he'd said.

'I am,' I said, teasing.

'Oh . . .'

I decided to change the subject quickly before the silly boy got upset. I *was* only teasing . . .

'So where *were* you all lesson?' I asked him.

'In the toilets . . .'

'The boys' . . . ?' I asked stupidly.

'Well I'm not gonna hide in the *girls'* toilets am I?' he grinned.

'Doesn't Mr Black check them . . ?'

'Yeah but the one time he came in I pretended I was using it . . .'

'So you spent an *hour* in the *loo*?' I replied, disgusted at the idea.

'Locked in a cubicle, yeah . . .' Jit said, as we made our way to English.

'You *stinky, stinky* boy . . .'

'Shut up Grace . . .'

Dean ignored all my efforts to find out where he had been all afternoon, telling me that it was personal and I had no right to know. Only he said it with a grin, so that I'd know he was winding me up. Which would only wind me up even more. Which, I *suppose*, was the whole point.

By the time we were walking down to get the bus I was offering Dean my personal Mini-Disc player for a week, on loan, if only he'd tell me where he'd been. He continued to say 'no' so I threw in some CDs too. Eventually, he grabbed my hand and pulled me to one side, out of earshot of the others.

'I'll come round later and tell you', he said. 'But only if you promise that you'll keep it a secret . . .'

I promised.

'I'll come by about seven-ish then . . .' added Dean.

'Cool,' I said, looking towards the rest of our friends and seeing Jit staring back at me.

I thought about asking Dean if we could let Jit in on the secret but realised that it might be amusing not to, for a few days at least. Not to be mean, or anything. Just to wind him up a bit. I started wishing time away as the bus crawled through the traffic, excited that I was about to share a secret with Dean. I loved secrets – they were so much fun . . .

SEVEN

I heard the phone ringing upstairs as Dean placed some pool balls in a row for the sixth time and attempted to show me what he called his 'killer' shot.

'See how the balls is all lined up and that? Well – if I hit the one at the end with the white ball then the one at the *other* end will double into that pocket there . . .' He pointed at one of the corner pockets.

'You said that last time and it didn't work. And the time before that . . .' I teased. 'Will it *ever* work, Dean?'

Dean gave me a withering look.

'GRACE!' shouted my dad from the top of the stairs. 'PHONE . . . !'

'You practice your shot, sonny, and I'll go see who's on the phone,' I told Dean, as he squinted at the balls.

I ran upstairs into the hallway and picked up the handset.

'Hello?'

'*Hi Grace . . . it's . . . er . . . me. What you doin'?*'

It was Jit.

'Not a lot . . . Dean's come over and he's showing me some pool shot or other.'

'*Dean? Oh . . . can I . . . ?*'

'You always do anyway,' I replied.

'*See you in a bit then . . . ?*' he asked, rather than said, which was unlike him.

'OK then you weirdo . . . can you stop by the shop and get me some Maltesers on the way?'

'*Er . . . yeah. If I can get some dough . . . I haven't . . .*'

'That's OK – I'll nip out and get some myself,' I said quickly, hoping that I hadn't embarrassed him.

'*Cool.*'

The line went dead. I put the handset in its cradle and went back down to the cellar where Dean was lining up his shot yet again.

'Are you going to get that right or are we gonna be here all night?' I said, smiling, as I sank into an armchair.

'Patience, man . . . you're watching an artist at work y'know . . .' replied Dean, taking the shot.

The ball that was supposed to end up in a pocket glanced off a cushion, missing by about three inches.

'So is that your secret then, Dean – that you can't play pool?' I asked, impatient for him to tell me about where he'd been earlier.

'I keep telling you, Grace. You ain't funny so don't bother wastin' your time . . .'

'Well if you're not going to tell me . . .'

'Who was on the phone?' he asked, changing the subject.

'Jit – he's on his way round so you'd better tell me quickly because otherwise I'll tell him that you're keeping secrets.'

'*Ehh* check you out . . . blackmail, man.'

I laughed at him and told him to shut up and tell me.

'Well it's like this, and I told you about this before, only you was too dumb to listen. I joined a social . . .'

'What?' I replied.

'A social. A lunchtime activity club. That way, even when I'm on late lunches, every Wednesday I get to leave Maths early and get a nice hot dinner instead of that concrete they keep for the late lunches . . .' Dean came and sat down on the sofa, pleased with himself.

'You joined a *nerd* society . . . ?' I said, wondering if he'd gone mad.

'Yeah . . . Chess Club, man. Why, what you sayin' – that I can't play chess if I want to . . . ?' replied Dean.

'You can play chess till your fingers drop off, you stinky boy,' I snorted. 'But I'm thinking that you didn't join to pick up tips on where the pawn goes . . .'

'Elementary, my dear Parkhurst . . . like that knob

Sherlock Holmes always says. I joined to get out of Maths early and to get a hot dinner . . .'

'So what did you do all lunchtime – talk about comics with nerdy kids . . . ?' I asked, imagining the conversations that might possibly come up.

'Yeah well, they *tried* to talk to me but I just told 'em to go away,' said Dean.

'So you didn't actually get involved or anything?'

Dean sat forward excitedly. 'Nah man! It's a blag innit? All I did was show up, sit at the back and move a few pieces around a board.'

'So who's the teacher in charge of it then?'

'That Wilson – the *Science teacher*? The one that looks like he needs a hot meal . . .'

'The skinny man who mumbles to himself?'

I'd seen him in the corridors, walking around like a twig in a lab coat.

'Yeah – *Willy* Wilson . . . and he didn't even notice me. He just came in, spoke to a couple of the top nerds and then left . . .'

'So you had *no* supervision and no one *checked* to see if you were actually there for the chess?' I asked, amazed *and* interested.

'*Exactly*, Sister Gee,' he replied.

I smiled and told him to call me Sister Gee again. I liked it – it made me sound like a female MC. Dean laughed along and then told me that I could join Chess Club if I wanted to.

'Anyone can join . . . it's just that most of the all right kids don't know about it. It's like a secret Harry Potter lookalike society . . . only for those in the know and that. Man you should have seen the looks on their faces when I showed up . . .'

'Can I register for it tomorrow?' I asked.

'Yeah – I just asked Miss Dooher about it and she gave me a list of activities . . .'

'There's no catch or anything . . . ?'

'Just two man. *One* – you get to leave lessons before everyone else and *two* – you get to eat a nice hot dinner or, in your case, a sandwich that don't look like it's been farted on by an elephant . . .'

'Why would an elephant fart flatten my sandwich . . . ?' I asked, giggling.

'Oh you know what I mean . . .' said Dean. 'So what do you reckon then . . . ?'

'I'm up for it,' I said as the door to the cellar opened and my dad called down. 'Grace – Jit's here . . . I'll send him down.'

As Jit came down the stairs I quickly finished my conversation with Dean.

'Cool – let's do that tomorrow . . .' I said, turning to smile at Jit.

'Do what?' he asked, looking from me to Dean.

'Nuttin' man,' smiled Dean. 'Just something that Grace and me gonna do.'

'What – like *together* . . . ?'

'Yes,' I told Jit. 'But don't worry – we aren't getting married or anything.'

I smiled as Jit raised an eyebrow and came over all confused. He really was a funny young man. He ignored me in the end and he and Dean played pool together as I watched telly. About an hour later Hannah came round with some homework and we tried to do that as the lads argued over free shots and stuff.

The next morning I signed up for the weekly Wednesday chess club and waited impatiently for the week to pass so that I could leave Maths early with Dean. I found Dean by the tennis courts at break, chatting up some girl.

'Done it!' I beamed at him, butting in on his conversation.

Dean told the girl that he would 'check for her' later and I asked what he was going to check her for. He grinned at me and told me to stop being a dickhead.

'You know,' he began, 'last night Jit was asking me about our secret all the way home, man.'

'Did you tell him?' I asked.

'Nah – let him sweat . . . I think he's got it wrong anyway. He probably thinks that you and me are going out or something . . .'

'URGH! No disrespect but you smell . . .'

'Hush up man – me have a bath *every* day – twice 'pon a Saturday.'

We laughed with each other as we walked over to the others, who were standing just inside the entrance to school. Jit gave us a strange look when he saw us and I realised that maybe Dean was right. Silly young man . . .

EIGHT

The following Wednesday Dean and I got up to leave Mrs Lee-Cross' Maths lesson with the nerds. Jit was sitting beside me and asked me where I was going but Mrs Lee-Cross told him to mind his own business and concentrate on the lesson in hand. He shrugged and whispered to me to tell him later. I smiled and followed Dean out of the room, aware of the funny looks that Hannah, Suky and Imi were giving us too. I so *loved* having a secret.

We went down to the dinner hall and I was amazed at the fresh-looking sandwiches laid out in front of me, all pristine and edible-looking. We were the first to arrive and by the time the lunch bell rang we were already eating ours.

'Come on,' said Dean, wolfing down some of his chips and wrapping the rest in a piece of bread, 'bring the rest with you. We don't want the others to see us and they're on first lunch.'

He got up to take his tray to the counter.

'Oh yeah – nearly forgot,' I said, grabbing the remains

of my sandwich and my apple and heading off after him.

We took a long route to the science block, so that we would avoid the others as they came in for lunch. Some of the other pupils from Chess Club were already there when we arrived, concentrating hard on their next moves. Dean mouthed the word 'sad' at me as we took a table at the back of the room, by the window. He unfolded the chess board in front of us and laid it out, taking the pieces out of their box.

'Man, I don't even know where these things are supposed to go . . .' he said, smiling mischievously.

'I've played before,' I admitted, rearranging the pieces so that they were on the correct squares.

'I should've guessed, man,' he told me. 'Grace Parkhurst – used to be a nerd but she all right now!'

'Get stuffed . . .' I replied, embarrassed.

'Nah – it's OK. Looks like an interestin' kinda game . . .'

'Don't laugh at me or I'll tell the others,' I warned.

'Oh yeah – er . . . sorry.'

I grinned and moved my first pawn. Dean looked at me like I was crazy.

'What you *doing* Grace? We ain't gonna actually *play* the game,' he said.

'We can pretend . . . that way we can have a chat and not look like we're just here to miss part of Maths and get an early lunch . . .'

'Yeah but that's why we are here,' replied Dean.

'*Ah* – but *they* don't know that, do they,' I told him, nodding at the rest of the Chess Club, which was being supervised by Mr Wilson.

He looked over at us and smiled shyly. I grinned back and, raising my voice, told him that I absolutely adored chess. Dean kicked me under the table.

'Grace . . . !' he whispered, giving me a filthy look, as Mr Wilson tottered over on his twiglet legs.

'And you are . . . ?' asked Wilson.

'Grace Parkhurst,' I beamed. 'And this is my friend Dean Chambers.'

'Well, hello and welcome to the Chess Club, people . . .' grinned Wilson, trying to act cool but coming off sounding like my dad.

'It's a really *cool* club. We've got a club challenge and a couple of videos about opening gambits and master tactics and next month we're entering the top two players in a challenge with another school. That'll be fun . . .'

Dean was looking at Wilson the way a cat looks at humans who talk to them – all incomprehension with a touch of bemusement thrown in.

'Yeah, *man*,' he replied, emphasising the 'man', 'the chess club sounds *groovy* . . .'

Wilson smiled at us as I struggled to hold down my giggles. I shot up and ran to the loo, not coming back until I'd cried with laughter, by which time Wilson had gone and Dean was busy rolling up bits of paper and flicking them at a lad called Wesley Magoogan who was good at anything that involved numbers but terrible at everything else. Wesley was ignoring the paper bullets that were constantly landing on his board. He was far too busy trying to beat his chess partner, Robert Sargeant, another of our year group's more socially-challenged pupils. Robert was just removing the paper as it landed, without even looking up at Dean.

'Dean – don't be such a bully . . .' I said, reprimanding him.

'I'm only playing . . .' he protested.

'Yeah but if they complain to Wilson he'll kick us out and bangs goes our little scam . . .' I pointed out.

'Good thinking Sister Gee – I'll stop.'

'So what do we do now then . . . ?' I asked.

'Let's write a rap, man . . .' said Dean, excitedly.

'A *rap* . . . ?'

'Yeah – you know – lyrics dat flow in a way dat you *know* will get the gal dem fe *crow* . . . !' said Dean without taking a breath.

'But I've never written a . . .'

'Come Sister Gee, man! I ain't gonna let you keep the name otherwise . . .'

I smiled and pulled a pad and a pen from my bag.

'But what if Wilson comes back . . . ?' I asked, as Dean grabbed my stationery.

'We'll just tell him that we're writing down the moves and that – to learn them . . .'

'Oh go on then,' I said, trying to think of words that rhymed in my head.

'Right – we need a topic to write about,' said Dean, doodling on a page of paper.

'What about the Chess Club?' I suggested.

'Nah – that's lame. What about something to do with school though – like Mr Herbert . . . ?'

'Mr Herbert? What could we possibly rap about him . . . ?' I asked.

Dean thought about it for a moment before replying.

'Dunno – what about his spots or his ratty face . . .' he said.

'Or the way he goes red in the face when he shouts . . . ?' I added, warming to the task.

'Yeah man!' shouted Dean, alerting the rest of the chess club.

'Ssh . . . !' came a joint whisper from the rest of the pupils in the room.

'Hush yuh mout' man . . .' replied Dean, harshly.

The rest of the club turned back to their games, most of them red in the face.

'Dean . . . !'

Dean gave me a shrug of his shoulders.

'What? They wanna mind them own, innit . . .'

'Ooh bad boy!' I replied, jokingly.

'Anyway like we was sayin' – Herbert . . .'

I was about to reply but Dean suddenly smiled to himself and started to write some words down on the paper. Five minutes later he proudly pushed the piece of paper in my direction, grinning from ear to ear. I picked it up and read the words that he'd written. I was amazed at how quickly he'd done it. 'Yuh see me?' he said, boasting. 'Me is the *Dan*!'

I finished reading it and looked at him.

'It's a bit lame, I reckon,' I said, teasing him.

His face dropped. 'What *you* know about it, anyway?' he said, kissing his teeth and dismissing me with a wave of his hand.

'Well – it's not like I even like rap . . .'

'Let me rap it to you – it's different to the way it seems when it's written down,' he told me.

'You're going to rap *here* – in Chess Club . . . ?' I asked.

'Yeah man – it ain't no big thing.'

Dean took the sheet of paper and stood up, clearing his throat and daring the rest of the club to tell him to shut up with one of his looks. They just sat where they were, bemused but interested all the same. Dean bowed and spoke . . . *'Yes people! Right now for your entertainment and pleasure MC D-C ah go give you the Herbert Rap . . .'*

Most of the club giggled and looked at each other. Dean smiled at me and cleared his throat again.

'See, geezer sits in his chair,
shoutin' like he just don't care.
But when him check out all the facts,
Geezers headin' fe a heart attack!

So chill Mr Teacher, chill out nuh man,
stop shouting at us, loud as you can.
Cos one day soon, and it's a fact,
You ago give yourself a heart attack!
Give yourself a heart attack!

Wid yuh red-up face and the hair you lack,
Sometimes you even smell kinda wack.
So just chill out geezer – give peace a try,
Cos if you don't – you might just die . . .'

The rest of the club sat where they were, grinning to each other, as Dean finished. I looked at him, smiled, and started to clap. One by one the nerds broke into laughter and clapped along, just as the afternoon registration bell rang. Dean grabbed his stuff and grinned like he'd won a prize or something. I got up, collected my things and followed him down to registration.

'Yeah, you were right,' I told him.

'See? Looks lame on paper but when you actually rap it . . .' Dean was saying, as we walked into the form room.

Mrs Dooher smiled at us and told us to have a sweet from a bag she had on her desk. Dean grinned, grabbed a sweet and then hugged Mrs Dooher.

'You is *soooo* lovely,' He gave her a kiss on her cheek. Mrs Dooher shook him off and went and sat down.

'You *little get*!' she said, smiling.

Jit walked in with the rest of the gang and they sat down.

'Where was you then?' he asked me.

'Nowhere,' I replied, trying to sound mysterious.

Jit shrugged his shoulders and turned away from me. 'Suit yourself,' he said, but not to my face.

All of a sudden I wasn't as pleased with myself. I'd upset him. '*Jit* . . . !' I whispered, as Mrs Dooher read out some notices.

He didn't reply and when the bell went he shot out of the classroom before anyone else. Hannah noticed and shook her head as we followed the others to classes.

'He's not a happy bunny, is he?' she said.

'I think I upset him . . .' I told her.

'Nah – he's just immature . . .' replied Hannah.

'*No he's not!*' I half shouted.

I don't know why but Hannah's comment had made me want to defend Jit. It was so not me. I went red in the face. But only for a moment.

'Calm down Grace,' Hannah said, smiling. 'Anyway – where *did* you and Dean get to over lunchtime . . . ?'

NINE

The others were asking me and Dean where we'd got to every five minutes for the rest of the day. In the evening I rang Jit, who told me that he was busy and couldn't come round, which was odd for him. I put it out of my mind until the next morning when he didn't turn up at the bus stop.

'Where's Jit?' I asked Dean as we got on the bus.

'Dunno.'

'Didn't you call for him?' I said, taking my ticket and following Dean upstairs, as the bus pulled away from the stop.

'Yeah – but no one answered the door. He's probably pretending to be ill or something . . .'

I looked down the road to see if he might be running, late for the bus, but there was no sign of him – just an old couple walking their poodle and a gang of older lads, including Jason Patel, who were making no effort to catch the last bus that would get them to school on time. I wondered why so many of the pupils who lived near Dean and Jit walked the fifteen minute journey to the stop near my house. It didn't make any sense at all but then they were all boys. Odd.

'I hope he's all right,' I told Dean, but he was busy taking something out of his bag.

'This is a list of all the other socials that you can go to,' he said, holding a folded sheet of A4 up.

'What, you mean we don't *have* to go to Chess Club on Wednesdays?' I asked, wondering what other delights were available.

'Nah, on Wednesdays Chess Club's the best one. These are for the rest of the week,' he replied, grinning.

'We can go to more than one lunchtime club?' I hadn't even considered that possibility.

'Well yeah – I *think* we can. I'm not sure that there's a limit or anything,' he said, evasively.

I took the piece of paper from him and opened it. On it was a box grid with the days of the week from Monday to Friday down one side and a list of the available clubs and activities against each day. At the top of the page, in bold type was a note that said we were only allowed to attend two of these socials in any given week. I held the note in front of Dean's face.

'You little liar . . . it says here that . . .'

Dean grinned even wider. 'That's the official rule but who's gonna check . . . ?' he asked me.

'Anyone. Mr Black or one of the other teachers. One of the other pupils even . . .' I pointed out.

'No one even bothered to check on us at the last one. There weren't no register taken was there?'

'Yes – but that doesn't mean another teacher won't take a register at one of the other socials,' I argued.

'Relax Grace, man. It ain't no big deal. I'm sure that them nerds go to more than they're supposed to anyway . . .'

I gave him a raised eyebrow. Yeah, like Wesley Magoogan and his mates were going to break the rules. Dean kissed his teeth at me.

'OK then – let's ask them . . .' he said, looking round for a suitable candidate. He didn't find one. Pupils like Wesley and Robert Sargeant were already at school by the time we caught our bus each morning. They caught the earlier one. Dean shrugged.

'We'll ask that Wesley later,' he said, 'and anyway – we can at least pick *one* more . . .'

I looked at the list of clubs and at the days on which they were available. Dean leaned over and pointed at the list for Thursdays.

'Thursdays we have English with Herbert, right? So if we pick one for that day we can get out his lesson ten minutes early – that'll wind him right up.' He sat back and smiled at me.

'But he'll get suspicious . . .' I said.

'He can't do *jack* though, can he? We're *allowed* to go to these things . . .'

'I dunno,' I said, 'I can see this ending in tears . . .'

'Grace – you sound like your dad, man. Leave it out. It's just a blag.'

'OK – so which one should we pick?' I asked, looking at the list.

Dean's grin stayed where it was, as though he'd fallen victim to that thing that your parents tell you when you're young about the wind changing direction and your face staying that way.

'I took the liberty,' he said, in what he would probably call a posh voice, 'of choosing for you m'dear . . .'

I gave him a look. 'I'm sorry . . . ?'

'I chose one for you already . . .' he repeated.

'*Dean* . . .'

'*Well* – I knew you'd be OK about it once I'd *told* you so I picked one for you. *Us* even . . .'

'Which one . . . ?' I asked, praying that he hadn't picked Science Club or Model Making, which were both on the list.

'Er . . . Science . . .'

'*DEAN!*' I shouted, and the whole top deck of the bus looked at us. Someone wolf whistled and shouted that we were having a lovers' tiff. I stuck my fingers up at them. Dean cracked up.

'Only kidding, Sister Gee, man. I picked the Book Club. We start today . . .'

I was about to say something but I stopped myself and thought about it. We were going to miss ten minutes of English every Thursday to go to a book club. Even Mr Herbert couldn't complain about that. And I love books. I might even enjoy it.

'OK – that's a good choice,' I said, smiling. '*But* you never read anything . . .'

'I can start, can't I?' replied Dean. 'And anyways it's *a blag*, Grace. A *blag* . . .'

Wesley was standing by the stairs that led up to the science block after registration, waiting for his friends. Dean and I had gone looking for him on the way to our first lesson. Jit hadn't turned up at school either but Hannah had brought in a note from his mum saying that he was ill and wouldn't be in school for a few days. I would have worried about him if Hannah hadn't produced the note but I was happy that he was ill. *Well*, not happy exactly, but relieved that it wasn't something else – like he was upset or in trouble with someone.

When Dean called out Wesley's name he went red and froze to the spot.

'Relax Wesley,' smiled Dean, 'I just want some advice, man.'

Wesley's shoulders relaxed and he slowly changed from beetroot to strawberry.

'What can I help you with . . . er . . . Dean . . . ?' he managed to say.

'It's about them socials and that,' replied Dean. 'You know, like the Chess Club thing . . .'

Wesley smiled, just a little. 'Oh yes . . .' he said.

'Well, is like this man,' began Dean, 'I wanna know if they ever take like a register at them things . . . you know does anyone ever check who's there and who's not?'

Wesley considered what Dean had said like it was some Maths problem that he'd been set. He looked at me, smiled just a little more and then cleared his throat as if he was about to say something really important

'Well, Mr Wilson comes in now and then but he doesn't—'

'And are you in any other clubs?' interrupted Dean.

Wesley went back to beetroot.

'Er . . . I . . . er . . .' he stammered.

I decided that it was time for a little feminine charm.

'Hi – *Wes* – can I call you Wes . . . ?'

'Um . . . er . . .' he replied. I was just waiting for him to say mummy.

'So, Wes, *do you* attend any other socials . . . ?' I continued, smiling at him.

He coughed and looked down at his feet.

'Yes . . . I er . . . attend Science Club on Thursdays,' he told us.

'Oh,' I whispered, moving closer to him and putting my hand on his arm. 'And what about any others?'

He looked at my hand like it was a claw on the end of the arm of some kind of monster.

'We're . . . we're not allowed to . . .'

I moved my face even closer to his, aware that Dean was smirking next to me.

'I know that Wes but you seem kind of clever to me . . . I'm *sure* someone like you knows *all kinds* of ways to avoid the rules. Come on . . . just between *us* . . .' I whispered.

Wesley started to edge backwards, away from my face but he came to the wall and had to stop. I moved further towards him, trapping him against the wall. He looked up at my eyes and gulped. I was dying to laugh but held it back.

'Well . . . ?' I said, almost into his ear.

'Yes . . . *yes!*' he shouted. 'I do attend more than I should . . . *I do . . . I do!*'

Dean started laughing really loudly then and it was

all I could do to stop myself from joining him. Wesley stepped away from me and told me the rest.

'I attend four a week,' he said. 'I know it's wrong but you won't tell anyone will you . . . ?'

'No, no Wes – this will be our little secret,' I replied.

'It's just that no one checks and it's all a bit of harmless fun . . .' he continued, smiling a little.

'Yeah – OK Wesley,' I said, 'I get the picture . . .'

Only Wesley didn't catch my drift and carried on talking. '. . . and Robert and I, we thought well what the . . .'

'Wesley.' said Dean.

'Er . . . yes?' he replied.

'Shut up . . . there's a good little boy.'

'Er . . . OK Dean. See you both in Chess Club?' he half-stated, half-asked.

'I can hardly wait,' I told him, in a breathless voice.

Wesley scampered off up the stairs and Dean poked me in the arm.

'Man, you are harsh . . . playing up to him like that.'

'I don't know *what* you mean,' I replied, smiling slyly.

'Man thinks he's in there . . .' laughed Dean.

'*Er yeah* . . . like in his wildest *dreams*.'

Later that morning, Dean and I left Mr Herbert's lesson early and the looks we got from Hannah, Imtiaz and

Suky told me that we were going to have to tell them about our scam very soon. All afternoon, they just talked amongst themselves hardly allowing Dean or myself to join in with their conversations. When I complained though, Dean laughed at me.

'Jealous, man. Don't worry about it . . .'

'But I *am* worried about it. They're our friends . . .'

'It's no big deal, Sister Gee . . .'

'We're going to have to tell them,' I said, more to myself. Dean had stopped listening to me and was busy telling me that we had to pick some more socials.

'. . . Fridays we get to miss some of CDT . . . Tuesdays we'll miss ten minutes of Geography . . . man this is wicked! *And* no more concrete chips ever again!'

I looked at him and shook my head. Stinky boy . . .

TEN

There was no sign of Jit the next morning either as Dean and I made our way to school. I had toast crumbs on my jumper and Dean was telling me to brush them off as we walked up to the school, late again. Mr Black was waiting at the gate, as usual, holding a clipboard.

'Good morning,' he said in a loud jolly voice as we meandered towards school.

'Morning sir . . .' both of us said in unison.

'Yes – and a fine morning too – sunny and bright with just a touch of autumn chill. Just the kind of morning on which I'd expect my pupils to be up bright and early. *Bright and early* . . .' he replied, looking at us inquisitively.

'Sorry sir . . .'

'*Sorry?* . . . You're not *sorry*. If you were anywhere approaching *sorry* you would attempt to get to school on time for a change,' he told us, without changing his tone.

I exchanged a look with Dean as Mr Black smiled away, like a demented puppet.

'You're going to have to learn that behind the motto lies iron will,' he told us, still smiling.

'Yes sir . . .' I said, wondering what he was on about. I didn't have long to wait to find out.

'Detention . . . from Monday evening Miss Parkhurst. That goes for you too Mr Chambers and the rest of this sorry band.'

He gestured with an arm towards the other pupils sauntering slowly up the road.

'*RIGHT!* Get in line the lot of you . . . !' he shouted breezily, as the other pupils moaned and complained.

'Name and form group on this clipboard please . . .' he told them all. 'In life you'll find that not many people are given the number of second chances that I allow my pupils. But then you know me – firm but fair. *Firm but fair.*'

A collective groan went up as I wrote my name and form number down on the clipboard before handing it to Dean, who looked at it as though I'd handed him a mouldy fish or something. He wrote down his details and we made our way to the door.

'Monday night, you two . . . assembly hall. One hour – you can let your parents know over the weekend. And the rest of you – don't bother to write down the names of imaginary pupils. I know who all of you are . . .' said Black, *still* smiling.

'What a lovely morning' he said again, to no one in particular, as Dean and I headed for our form room.

We arrived to find Mrs Dooher in a bad mood. Well bad for her anyway. She wasn't smiling at all and she had already taken the register when we joined the gang.

'I've got a note here from Mr Black . . .' she said, standing up, 'about late attendances.' She looked at Dean and myself. 'And I believe that you two are the prime offenders.'

'But Miss—' Dean began only to be cut off.

'But nothing Dean . . . there's always an excuse . . .'

'The bus don't come until whenever and then there's always traffic and that . . .' he continued, unfazed.

'Yes – the infamous "late bus" said Mrs Dooher with more than a touch of sarcasm. 'The only problem with that theory is that our wonderful Principal has undertaken to *time* when it arrives at the stop. And he *also* timed how long it takes to walk from said bus stop to the school gate . . .'

'Man's a weirdo,' laughed Imi.

'He may well be, but he does have a point,' said Mrs Dooher. 'That particular bus, the 42, gets to the stop fifteen minutes before you are due at school. It's no more than a five minute walk from the stop to the school gates so somewhere there's a missing ten minutes . . .'

Someone shouted out '*DUN DUN DERRR!*' at the

idea of the mysterious missing minutes and Mrs Dooher broke into a grin.

'Whatever the ins and outs,' she continued, 'the upshot of this is that anyone who is late from now on will be subject to detention in the assembly hall on Monday evenings . . .'

'Huh?' asked Suky, looking at Hannah.

'Yeah – like what if you're late on a Wednesday?' added Imi.

'Then you will have to put your name on the clipboard at the gate and attend mass detention the following Monday . . .'

'That's just mad, that is . . .' said Suky.

'Mass detention . . . what we gonna get next Miss – army induction training before chemistry . . . ?' Hannah asked

'And what about people who are late every day . . . ?' asked a boy called Dilip from the back.

Everyone looked at me and Dean. I went red and looked down at the desk. Dean just shrugged and grinned.

'Yeah,' added Imi, 'how is that fair? If I'm late one day and someone *else* –' he pinched Dean in his side. Dean wriggled but stayed quiet, still grinning '– is late every day, then I get the same punishment as *that* person,' he finished, pointing at Dean.

'Calm down class . . . the whole point of the exercise is to weed out the *persistent* offenders,' Mrs Dooher told us, reading straight from Mr Black's note.

'Yeah but it ain't fair is it . . . ?' continued Imi. 'Just because some of us are mature enough to get to school on time and some aren't – why should we all suffer . . . ?'

'But if you're not late then why would it bother you, Mr Dhondy?' pointed out Mrs Dooher. Imi shrugged, conceding the point.

'Still not fair,' said Suky, backing up Imi, like she always did.

Mrs Dooher was about to say some more but the bell for first lesson went and everyone groaned and stood up, grabbing their stuff.

'School's *nuts* man,' said one pupil.

'*Principal's* nuts,' said another. 'That's what my dad reckons . . . imagine calling it Devana High and then getting that nutter to run it . . .'

'*My* dad,' said a third pupil, a girl called Heather, 'reckons that Mr Black used to take loads of drugs in the Sixties and that . . .'

'*Whass the Sixties?*' asked Dilip, looking confused, as Mrs Dooher ushered us off to our lessons.

At break Hannah and I were sitting on the steps that led up to the tennis courts, watching the older boys playing football. There was one in particular, a lad in Year 10 called Billy who we both thought was fit. Hannah was watching him as he played, but my mind was on Jit and what was wrong with him. I was trying to get Hannah to pay attention to me and it was hard going.

'Are you listening to me?' I asked for the fifth time.

'Yeah – course I'm listening. I can do more than two things at the same time you know.'

'Yes – but are you paying attention . . . ?'

'Not quite in the way that you'd like me too, no,' she said with a grin.

'Hannah!'

'What . . . ? Oh . . . Jit. Look, I went round to see him last night.'

'*And?*' God, she was winding me up.

'And what? He opened the door and stood there like a weirdo. Didn't even invite me in.'

'Did he look sick?' I asked.

'Depends on what you mean by sick I suppose,' she replied, not looking at me.

'What's that supposed to mean? How many ways are there to look sick . . . ?'

'Hmmm?' she mumbled, twisting round so that she could watch Billy from a better angle.

'Hannah!'

Hannah finally turned to look at me.

'What? Er . . . he looked normal. There wasn't like a big sign on his forehead saying "living dead" or anything. He just stood there and asked me what I wanted . . .'

'And . . . ?'

'Man! You fancy him or something?'

'No!' I protested.

'Just, the way you've been with Dean lately anyone would think that you and *him* had something going on . . .' she added, turning her full attention to me now that Billy had walked off with his mates.

'What you on about?'

'Well. All that going around in secret and leaving lessons and stuff – what's that all about?' she asked.

'Nothing – you'll find out soon enough. You could say we're doing some research for everyone else. Kind of testing the water . . .' I winked at her.

'Yeah – what*ever* . . . anyway Jit was his usual strange self. You know – rude, mardy . . .'

'Did you ask him if he was ill, Hannah?'

'Yeah – he said he had a cough and then he told me that he wanted to go to bed and shut the door in my face.'

I gave her a surprised look. She saw it and shrugged.

'Don't worry – he's fine. I've told you so many times

Grace – he's a nutter. *Lovely* but nuts – ever since he was a kid. He gets really quiet sometimes . . .'

Something in my nosy investigator head perked up and took notice. 'Why do you think he's like that then?' I asked.

Hannah shrugged and looked away for a moment. Without looking back she said something about him having had a rough time as a kid. I was sure she knew more than she was letting on but I let it go. After all, followed by Dean, she was Jit's oldest and closest friend. She was bound to know more about him that anyone else. I just wanted to know too, but not if Jit didn't tell me himself.

'That Billy is lovely,' said Hannah, changing the subject. She got up and wiped her clothes down.

'He's all right,' I said, standing up too, ready to go back to lessons.

'Yeah – you wouldn't mind if he asked you out to the pictures . . .'

I smiled as we headed indoors. 'I'd tell him that my diary was full,' I insisted.

'I bet . . .' Hannah said, and laughed.

In the next lesson, History, Dean passed me a note. I waited for Mr Woods to turn to the board before I opened it.

'On Fridays it's Computer Club! Let's join up! What do you think . . . ?'

I looked at Dean and smiled. Imi saw me and asked me, in a whisper what was in the note.

'Nothing,' I whispered back.

'Yeah – looks like it,' he replied, just a little too loudly.

'Imtiaz . . . something to share?' asked Mr Woods.

'Er . . . no sir,' he replied, looking down at his pad of A4 and doodling.

I winked at Dean and nodded my head. 'In for a penny', as my dad was always saying . . .

ELEVEN

I spent most of Saturday morning trying to ring Jit. My dad was busy and my mum was away. Hannah came round at lunchtime to do some school work. She'd called for Jit on the way to mine. No one had answered again. By the time that we'd finished our school work it was mid-afternoon. I decided that I would ride back to Hannah's on my bike so that I could call for our missing friend, something that I'd only done three times before in all the time I'd known him. Hannah told me that I was mad.

'There's nothing up with him – nothing *physical* anyway,' she told me, as we walked back to hers.

'I just want to see if he's all right,' I protested, wondering why she thought it was such a big deal.

'That's probably what he wants you to do – it's just an act with him . . .' replied Hannah.

'Why would he put on an act?' I asked.

'Come on, Grace. It's obvious he likes you, but he has to be the centre of attention all the time. He's still a baby really . . .'

'He *doesn't like me* . . .' I said, not really believing my own words.

'Yes he does and you've been spending loads of time with Dean. I reckon he's just a little bit jealous,' she told me, smiling and shaking her head at the confused look on my face. Mainly because she knew that I was putting it on.

'It was only a bit of fun – we were going to tell you all about it . . .'

'Yeah . . . whatever,' smiled Hannah. 'Knowing Dean it's gonna be some crack-head scheme . . .'

'Don't you mean crack pot?' I asked, frowning.

'No Grace – I mean crack-*head* . . .'

We both giggled.

'Seriously though, he doesn't *fancy* me . . . not Jit.'

'Grace – you *know* that he does and I think that you like him too . . .' This time Hannah grinned alone.

'Don't,' I protested.

'Do,' she answered.

'Don't!'

'DO! Do-do-do-do-do!'

I gave Hannah a funny look. An Asian couple walking past gave her the same look. As did an old white woman walking her dog. Even the *dog* gave her . . . well *OK* . . . maybe not the dog.

'God, that was like back to primary school, wasn't it?' she asked me, embarrassed.

'Yes,' I told her. 'Infants even . . .'

We walked up onto a main road, past a huge mosque and an infant school. Hannah's house was still five minutes walk away and Jit's another five minutes after that. I realised again just how far Jit walked in the mornings to catch the same bus as me. Hannah and I had walked for fifteen minutes just to get to where we were.

'He's quite fit,' I said completely out of the blue, as we arrived at Hannah's street.

'Who?' she asked me, looking around to see who I was on about.

'Jit . . . well, he will be fit – when he's matured a bit . . .'

Hannah grinned again.

'*See*? Told you . . .'

'I don't fancy him *now*,' I said, 'but I can see that I might – you know – when we're like in Year 10 or something . . .'

'He *is* good looking,' agreed Hannah before screwing up her face. 'I couldn't go *out* with him though – he's like my brother.'

'Not now . . . but I can see why girls might fancy him . . .' I continued, not really knowing where I was going with my point.

'And you're as weird as he is. What do you mean you can see how he might be fit – you fancy him. You *already* think he's fit . . .' laughed Hannah.

'Yeah – but I wouldn't go out with him – I don't want a boyfriend yet . . . it's just too . . .'

'*Normal?*' asked Hannah, having a joke at my expense.

'Get lost,' I replied.

'I am,' she told me. 'See you Monday.'

She walked down the street to her house as I got on my bike and set off for Jit's. When I arrived at his mum's house the curtains were drawn and I could hear music coming from inside. Ragga. I pressed the bell and waited. When there was no reply after a few moments I pressed it again. Across the street a group of lads wolf whistled and asked me if I was checkin' anyone. I ignored them and rang the bell again, following up the ring with a firm knock on the door. The music went off and I heard someone moving about. I waited impatiently as the door opened and Jit stuck his head out, blinking at the daylight that flooded in. He looked surprised to see me.

'Er . . . hi Grace,' he said, sheepishly as I stood there.

'Hi!' I replied, cheerfully. 'Just thought I'd come round and see what was up with you . . .'

'Yeah . . . er . . . I'm fine. Just had bit of a cold, that's all,' he told me.

'Oh. You don't look like you've got a . . .' I began, before thinking better of it and changing the subject. 'So, can I come in or something?'

Jit looked confused for a moment before he spoke. 'Er . . . look why don't we go back round to yours,' he replied quickly.

I looked at him like he was mad.

'It's just that my mum's asleep and . . .'

'But you just had your music on dead loud,' I pointed out.

'Er . . . look can we please just go round to yours – the house is a mess and . . .'

'Yeah, yeah. OK,' I said, relenting. 'I suppose we can head back to mine – but you're a very strange boy.'

I smiled at him. Jit looked away and mumbled something about grabbing his jacket. He closed the door on me and went off, returning a few moments later wearing a jacket and with slightly dampened hair. I think that he'd sprayed some deodorant too judging by the smell coming from him.

'Are you OK . . . ?' I asked.

'Yeah!' he replied, as we walked back down the street.

'Weirdo . . . anyone would think you had something hidden at your house the way you go on.'

'It's nothing – I told you. The house is a mess and I was feeling a bit embarrassed and—'

'Yeah, whatever. You don't need to explain to me . . .' I interrupted, sweetly.

I did want to know why he wouldn't let me in but at the same time I didn't want to embarrass him any more than he obviously was already. We walked down the main road, past Hannah's street, and back down towards the mosque where we took the left-hand fork in the road, crossed over and walked down to Holmfield Road which led back towards where I lived. As we walked into Holmfield I saw a group of lads ahead of us, heading away from us. One of them was Jason Patel. I looked anxiously at Jit.

'It's Jason,' I said.

Jit nodded. Without speaking we both quickly turned first left to make a slight detour to my road, not speaking until we'd made it safely to my house, both of us relieved at avoiding another run-in with the nutter.

I led the way inside as my dad emerged from the front room, which was his study.

'Ah Jit! Just the man. I wonder could you help me with a little problem . . . ?'

'Er . . . yeah – go on then,' replied Jit, smiling for the first time since I'd knocked on his door.

'Great! Come in to the office . . .' said my dad, as we both followed him in.

His office was its usual messy self with books and

papers lying on every surface, including the wooden floor. In fact it was hard to make out that the floor *was* wooden. I only knew because I lived in the same house. My dad cleared a space around his rickety desk, supported under two of the legs by hardback books. It looked like it would be refused for firewood – the piece of junk! The walls were bare except for a couple of posters and a photo of my dad with some old guitarist called Mick Jones, who my dad idolised. I didn't even know who he was. One of dad's designs was lying on the desk top and Jit moved closer to take a look at it.

'I'm working on that right now,' Dad said, 'but that's not what I wanted your help with . . .'

'Dad?'

'Relax Grace – it's just something that I wanted to run by Jit. And you too . . .' he added quickly.

'What is it Mr Parkhurst?' asked Jit, curious.

'I'm considering replacing my stereo system, Jit. The one I've got is something that I bought before Grace was born and I've been reading up about these new systems . . . you know – all singing, all dancing type affairs . . .'

He beamed at Jit. Jit looked at me with amusement. I groaned and shrugged.

'Dad!'

'Come on Grace – it'll be fun,' replied my dad, pulling a pile of magazines from under his desk.

'I've got *What Hi-Fi, Hi-Fi Weekly*, a couple of dealer catalogues and some reviews from the Internet,' he said proudly.

My dad was a firm believer in good research. When our last telly had blown up he'd borrowed a black-and-white portable from my uncle and then spent three months trying to decide which new telly to buy. Three months of watching everything in gloomy, dull, black and white. Even the comedies looked like melodramas on that thing. Eventually he'd settled for this huge thing with digital integration and surround sound and all this other stuff that excited Jit and Dean. Boy's toys.

'Cool,' said Jit.

I sighed. It looked like I was going to have to wait to find out what was up with him.

'You'll stay for dinner obviously, Jit?' beamed my dad.

'Er . . . If that's all right,' replied Jit, unsure of himself and looking to me for confirmation.

'You always do anyway . . .' I said, shaking my head and smiling.

'Lovely – I think we'll get a takeaway – just remember to let your mum know,' my dad told him, opening the first magazine. 'Now what do you think to this ensemble . . .'

* * *

In the end Jit and my dad spent three hours trying to work out which system would be best, while I went off and watched TV, which was boring. The only things on were game shows and competitions where talentless idiots attempted to convince old people with long hair and sunglasses that they should allow them to make pop music. I ended up watching a documentary on the contribution of immigrants to Britain's culture and economy, taking notes to impress my teachers with. There was a whole section on Leicester too, so as I watched I tried to see if I could recognise streets and shops and stuff. Jit and my dad came in around eight o'clock and plumped themselves down on a sofa.

'Right Jit – what shall we have for dinner?' said my dad.

'You might as well adopt him and be done,' I replied, a little annoyed that I hadn't been asked what I wanted for dinner.

'Come on now Grace, there's no need for that – Jit's a guest in our house not to mention one of your best friends . . .' said my dad.

'Yeah – sorry,' I offered. 'It's just that he came round to see *me* and you borrowed him all night for your silly research thing . . .'

My dad got up, came over, ruffled my hair and then gave me a kiss, all the while saying 'Poor Gracey' in a silly voice.

'GERROFF!' I giggled as he tickled me.

In the end I fell off the sofa I was on and lay on the floor. Red faced and with tears in my eyes. I looked up at Jit who was smiling and stuck my tongue out at him. My dad left the room and came back a few moments later with takeaway menus – Chinese, Indian, and Italian. We opted for Chinese and ordered it. The takeaway was around the corner from the house so Jit and I waited ten minutes and then walked round to pick it up. I asked him what was up with him as we sat in the takeaway, getting hungrier and hungrier as the smell of food emerged from the kitchen at the back.

'It's just that you and Dean have been ignoring me,' he replied, after a while, not looking at me.

'We haven't been *ignoring* you – we've just been . . . *researching* something,' I told him.

'What?' he asked, picking at the edge of a magazine with his finger and thumb.

'Nothing . . . It's still a secret . . .' I said.

'*See*? You two are keeping secrets from me . . .' he protested.

'Jit – honestly it's nothing . . .'

'I don't believe you,' he said, in a sullen tone.

'*God*! You're like a kid sometimes . . .' I practically shouted.

The woman behind the counter looked at us for a moment and then smiled and continued to read her magazine. Jit sat for a while and then he looked at me.

'So tell me what it is if it's not such a big thing . . .' he said.

'Oh all right then . . . it's those socials that Dean was on about – you know all that stuff about missing late lunches and concrete chips and . . .'

I explained it all to him as we waited for the food order, and then on the short walk home, we came up with a little trick that we could play on Dean. That seemed to cheer Jit up and by the time my dad gave him a lift home at ten o'clock he seemed to be in a really good mood and told me that he'd see me on Monday morning. I thought back to what Hannah had said about Jit wanting to be at the centre of things all the time and decided that she had been right. But she was wrong about him fancying me . . . stinky pants girl.

TWELVE

The following Wednesday morning we were all sitting in Maths with Mrs Lee-Cross working on maths problems that she'd set. Jit held up his hand halfway through the lesson and when Mrs Lee-Cross asked what he wanted he told her that he needed to talk to her in private. She gave him a concerned look and then asked him to accompany her out into the corridor. Jit got up and followed her, not looking at any of us. As soon as the door closed behind them the entire class started to chat amongst themselves, beginning quietly and then raising their voices when they didn't hear the usual 'Shut up' command from the teacher. Dean was the first one of our group to make a comment on Jit.

'He's skivin' again, man,' he said to no one in particular.

'His business. He's the one gonna be stuck at the end of the year asking us to help him with his work,' replied Imtiaz.

'Well he wasn't well last week,' I chipped in, defending him.

Yeah right – he's *desperately* ill,' laughed Suky.

'He's a weirdo – I keep telling you,' added Hannah.

I looked away from them, trying not to grin. Mrs Lee-Cross came back in a few minutes later and asked the class to quieten down. She had this look on her face that was a cross between embarrassment and concern and I wondered what Jit had said to her.

We spent the rest of the lesson going over the problems that we had been set and ten minutes before the end Mrs Lee-Cross nodded at Wesley and Robert. They stood up and Dean and I used that as our cue to leave too. Hannah sighed as we left and called us part-timers.

'That'll be enough, Miss Meadows,' said Mrs Lee-Cross. 'Perhaps you could talk us through the next problem . . .'

I followed Dean to the dinner hall where we both grabbed some food and I watched as Dean threw his chips and beans down his throat. He might as well have tipped the whole plate down there he ate them so fast. I kept my sandwiches for the club and we were outside the Chess Club room before the bell had gone for lunch. I stopped at the door, looked in, and then turned to Dean.

'Ooh, we've got a new boy,' I said, smiling.

'Nice one! Another lamb to the slaughter . . .' laughed Dean, 'Which nerd we got this week then?'.

He opened the door and I waited for him to enter but he just stood where he was, his mouth wide open like a tunnel.

'How the . . . ?' he began as I broke into laughter.

'Yes Dean!' shouted Jit. 'I thought I'd come check out the nerd zone, innit.'

Dean turned to me and started to say something else only I interrupted him.

'I had to tell him, Dean. He forced it out of me . . . honest!' I lied, smiling as widely as I could.

'So what do you do with these things then?' asked Jit, picking up a knight.

Wesley smiled at me and started to explain the role of the knight and its position on the board only for Jit to hold up his hand and cut him off.

'I'm asking my devious friend over there – not you,' he told Wesley, whose face went bright red.

'Who yuh a call devious, man?' asked Dean, aggressively.

'You!' replied Jit in the same tone.

Both of them squared up to each other and the rest of the group froze, thinking that there was going to be a fight. I thought so too until I saw the smiles break on both their faces.

'You is one devious man, bro',' laughed Jit, throwing the chess piece at Dean, who ducked as it whistled past him.

From behind us came a plopping sound and an 'Oh'. We turned to see Mr Wilson standing in the doorway, with splashes of coffee on his glasses. Jit had somehow managed to get the piece to land in Wilson's coffee mug.

'All right, sir,' smiled Dean as Mr Wilson wiped off his glasses on his lab coat.

'Er . . . yes I'm absolutely fine,' replied Wilson, 'er . . . I'm afraid that I can't recall your . . .' He looked at Dean quizzically.

'It's Dean, sir,' replied Dean, still smiling. 'Dean . . . Patel . . .'

'Well, Mr Patel, it's time you got down to some chess, isn't it?'

Jit and me grinned at Dean's joke and then started to put the pieces on the boards. Well, I put them on the board. Jit was trying to get them to do rude things to each other.

'Jit!' I said, shaking my head. 'That's so childish . . .'

'Yeah, Jit,' smiled Dean, joining us, 'when you gonna grow up and be mature boy, innit?'

'I never knew Imi had a twin brother,' replied Jit, removing the Queen's head from the King's backside.

'We gonna tell *them* too, I suppose?' said Dean, looking at me.

'We should – they're our friends. It'll be fun, all of us

in Chess Club and Book Club and God knows what else . . .'

Jit gave Dean another of his looks.

'What – you mean you're in more than one?' he asked.

'Yeah,' replied Dean. 'Didn't the world's worst secret agent, *Double-OH-Nuttin*, tell you . . . ?'

'When's that?'

'Thursdays and then on Fridays it's computers and that . . .'

Jit smiled. 'Yes man! No more late lunches . . . let's sign up for everything, bro',' he said excitedly.

'We'll have to be careful that we don't get caught,' I said, cautiously.

'Why?' asked Dean. 'We're on detention every Monday for the rest of the year *anyways* – what else can they do?'

I thought about it and realised that he was probably right. We'd been late every morning that week and were due at the mass detention the following Monday anyway. And no doubt there would be more too. Then a sly grin spread across my face.

'We don't ever have the same teacher before lunch twice do we?' I said.

Jit and Dean thought about it for a moment and then agreed.

'Right,' I continued, 'and no one takes a register or anything . . . ?'

'Yeah,' they both said.

'So what's to stop us joining a club for *every* lunchtime?'

They looked at each other and then both of them grinned at the same time.

'*See*? They say it's the kids like us that cause all the fuss but when you check it – it's the nice, cute *posh* girls that get *us* into trouble . . .' laughed Dean.

'What if we do get caught?' added Jit.

I smiled. 'No problem – I'll just tell my dad that you led me astray . . .'

For a moment Jit thought that I was being serious.

'You can't do that, man . . . he'll batter me,' he replied.

'Like I would tell him,' I said. 'And anyway – he'd just laugh and say that you were a lad, Jit. He's softer on you than he is on me . . . and he lets you pick what we're going to eat . . .'

'What?' asked Dean, confused.

'Private joke,' I said, trying to wink at Jit and failing.

Dean did the exact opposite to what Jit would have done if I'd have said that to him. He told me to take my private joke and stuff it. Jit would have just gone mardy for the rest of the day. Someone told us to keep the noise down, but when we turned to see who it was, everyone was staring at their own games.

'Nerds, man . . .' laughed Jit, smiling at me like I had just given him a million pounds. In cash. Boys . . . !

THIRTEEN

We missed ten minutes of English with Mr Herbert the following day and ten minutes of Design and Technology on the Friday morning. By the time we were all leaving to go home, Hannah, Suky and Imi were really mardy with us. At the bus stop they stood separately from us and when Dean tried to get Imi to listen to his 'Herbert Rap', Imi moved away and told him that he wasn't interested. Not that it stopped Dean, who rapped it anyway, entertaining the rest of the pupils waiting for the bus. They liked it so much that some of them got Dean to repeat the lyrics over and over so that they could learn it too and eventually there were about twenty kids rapping along, as the bus made its way through the school-run traffic. Not that the other three heard it. They had sat on the lower deck to avoid us and I seemed to be the only one bothered by it.

'We have to tell them,' I told Jit. 'They're not stupid – they'll work it our soon enough . . .'

'How? The socials are like a secret nerd society. Man,

I bet Wesley and them have special handshakes and that . . .' replied Jit, unfazed.

'It's not a joke, Jit. I'm telling them . . .'

'When?' said Jit, smiling at Dean.

'Tonight – *now* . . . !' I replied, getting up and walking down the stairs as the bus rounded a corner. Not the cleverest thing to do.

I stumbled down the stairs onto the lower deck, ignored the laughter from the back and sat down on Hannah's knee.

'*Gerroff you nutcase*!' she screamed as I kissed her on the cheek.

'Come round later,' I said, smiling. 'There's something that I want to tell you.' I looked at the seat behind where Suky and Imi were pretending that I didn't exist.

'I want both of you to come too!' I beamed.

They looked at each other and ignored me.

'*Please* . . . !' I begged. 'Please, please, please!'

'Why?' asked Suky.

'I want to tell you what me and Dean have been up to . . .' I replied.

'What makes you think that we care?' asked Imtiaz, screwing up his face.

'Because if you *didn't* care then you wouldn't be such mardy arses about it, ignoring us and sitting downstairs . . .'

'Maybe we just want to act our ages for a change . . . ?' said Imtiaz.

'Oh get a sense of humour, idiot boy!' I told him, grinning. 'Come round at six . . . I'll get dad to make dinner for us all . . .'

'Yeah all right,' replied Hannah, 'but gerroff me will you – my leg's going to sleep.'

'Okey cokey,' I said in a stupid girlie voice. 'See you all later . . .'

Hannah grinned. Suky smiled and Imi shrugged his shoulders. I knew they'd turn up though. They always did.

We had vegetable lasagne for dinner and my dad was really off on one, telling the gang all about his new stereo, which he could link up to his laptop to download MP3 files from the Internet, and which included a mini-disc player and loads of other gadgets which might as well have been from another planet as far as I was concerned. I eventually got him to stop talking about it around seven o'clock. We went down to the cellar as my dad started to collect the dishes, a sullen look on his face, like I'd spoiled his party or something. My mum just laughed and called him a child, as she went off to the living room to relax after work.

Down in the cellar, Dean and Jit racked up the pool

balls and started to play as Imtiaz and the girls sat on the sofa and waited for me to tell them what had been going on.

'OK, mardy bums – the reason I asked you to come round was to tell you about what Dean and I have been up to,' I told them, smiling.

Imtiaz pretended to yawn and Suky looked at her hands. Hannah was watching Dean and Jit play pool. Not the reaction that I was hoping for.

'*Well* . . . ?' I said.

'Well *what*?' replied Imi.

'Ask me about it then . . .' I urged, convinced that they *did* care.

'All right – how is *it*?' asked Suky with a sad attempt at humour.

'Doh! Nice try . . .' replied Jit, waiting for Dean to take his shot.

'Get stuffed, Bhangra Boy,' she replied in turn, forcing a smile out of Hannah.

'Oh get on with it,' Imi said, sounding bored.

'We've been researchin' man,' Dean told them, unconcerned that he had just missed his shot by a couple of inches.

'Yeah – researchin' yer ass,' said Hannah.

'Is that how you got it, *yeah*?' Dean asked her, grinning.

'Oh for God's sake – what are you on about?' said Suky, raising her voice.

'*Well*, you know how Dean was complaining about having to go to late lunches . . . ? We've found a way to get out of them. Forever . . .'

'Is this the important thing you had to tell us?' asked Imtiaz. 'Man, that's so lame . . . who cares?'

'So you're quite happy to eat concrete chips and warm sandwiches and that?' Jit replied.

'Well no, but it ain't going to ruin my life or nothing . . .' said Imtiaz.

'Depends on what you eat,' added Dean. 'I seen this thing on the telly 'bout food poisoning and that . . . food can kill you, you know . . .'

'Shut up, Dean . . .' said Suky.

'Easy, sister . . .' laughed Dean.

'Oh shut up all of you!' I shouted. 'I'm trying to tell you something.'

Everyone looked at me in surprise. Surprise and just a touch of amusement. I ignored them and carried on.

'We found out about these lunchtime socials that the school runs. Clubs that you can go to from Tuesday to Friday. Dean joined one and then so did I and they're cool . . .'

'Socials?' asked Hannah, raising her eyebrows.

'Yeah, like Book Club and Computers . . .' I replied.

'*And* Chess,' grinned Jit. 'Don't forget to tell them about Chess . . .'

'*Chess* . . . ?' said Imtiaz, looking disgusted.

I looked at him and then at the girls.

'Er . . . yeah . . . Chess too . . . anyway. The thing is – if you join one of these clubs then you get to leave the lesson beforehand about ten minutes early so that you can get your dinner and then get to the club . . .'

'Hot food my friends – every day . . . *believe!*' added Dean, like he was talking about treasure.

'And the teacher can't say anything about it because they're like part of the social life of the school . . . only no one knows about them. No one cool anyway . . .'

'Yeah,' agreed Jit, 'they're like the home of nerds, man. Wesley and Robert go to them but they're open to everyone . . .'

'And that's where you've been disappearing off to?' asked Suky.

'Yes,' I told her.

'And you can go to one every day . . . ?' she continued.

'Well not on Mondays because they don't run then. And actually, strictly speaking, you can only join two . . .' I replied, looking to Jit and Dean for support.

'Yeah but no one don't check or anything,' added Dean.

'*Doesn't* check, Chambers . . .' scolded Hannah, mocking him, but getting it wrong herself, too.

'Ehh! Check out *Likkle Miss Dictionary* . . . chill man. Don't get all discombobulated or nothin'.'

Everyone stopped what they were doing and looked at Dean.

'*Dis-com-what-a-lated*?' asked Imi, amazed.

'And you reckon *I've* swallowed a dictionary,' grinned Hannah.

'What's it mean anyway?' said Jit.

'Bet he don't even know . . .' laughed Suky.

'Course I do, man. I man is the lyrics officer . . . words is my business . . .' replied Dean.

'So tell us what it means . . .' insisted Imtiaz.

'It means upset, man. Or uncomfortable . . .' Dean told him, proudly.

'Man, you really *are* spending too much time with Wesley Magoogan,' said Hannah, grinning again.

'Getting back to the socials – are you saying that we can join one every day?' asked Suky.

'Yes,' I replied. 'There's no register taken and the teachers just turn up and say hello before running off to do whatever . . .'

'It's a blag, man . . . no worries,' added Jit.

'But surely someone will work it out . . . ?' asked Imtiaz, suddenly interested.

I smiled.

'See – I knew it would get your attention,' I told him. 'So far we've joined three – but this week coming we're going to join one more . . .'

'You're mad,' said Hannah. 'You'll get caught.'

'So what?' replied Dean. 'We're on detention every Monday anyway . . . what else can they do . . . ?'

'And you never have to go for late lunch again . . . ?' asked Suky.

'No late lunch, no getting wet in the rain, no freezing to death, huddled up against a wall in Winter . . . heaven,' I told her.

'And the clubs ain't that bad either,' said Jit, supporting me. 'It'll be a right laugh if we all join the same ones . . .'

'I dunno,' Imtiaz said. 'It's OK to talk about it but what if we get caught . . . ?'

'We ain't just talking are we?' Dean reminded him. 'We've researched it . . . and Wesley and the nerds get away with it so why shouldn't we?'

'You mean they go to more than they should?' asked Hannah, amazed.

'Yes – we were shocked too,' I replied. 'Wesley breaking the rules . . . kind of strange but true. I asked him myself . . .'

'I bet he nearly wet his pants . . .' Imi said, laughing.

'Urgh! You stinky boy . . .' I said, screwing up my face. That wasn't an image I wanted in my head – thank you *very* much.

'So you lot gonna join or what . . . ?' asked Dean.

'Hush up and take your shot . . .' Jit told him.

'Stand back then, little boy. Watch how a big man play the game . . .'

I grinned at the gang.

'I'm going upstairs to ask your mum for a dictionary,' said Hannah.

'Why?' I asked.

'To check out Dean's big word . . . bet he's lying,' she told me.

'*Check it, check it, cos you know you can't test it . . .*' rapped Dean, missing his shot by a mile.

FOURTEEN

Imtiaz, Suky and Hannah joined the Chess Club first, coming along the following Wednesday. The look on Mrs Lee-Cross' face when we all got up to leave Maths was a picture, but she didn't try to stop us. Instead she said that she was pleased that young people were willing to take up such an ancient and exciting game. I barely kept my snigger under my breath as we walked out and headed for the dining hall with her still talking about it. The club was in full flow when we got there and no one said anything at all about our being there, not even Willy Wilson, who congratulated Dean on bringing him 'fresh troops' as he called the gang.

'Well done, Mr Patel,' he said, walking out of the room just as Hannah and Suky were about to tell him that Dean's surname was actually Chambers.

'What's that all about?' they asked me as Dean tried to play a game against Wesley and Robert.

'Just a little joke . . .' I replied. 'So – what do you think then?'

'It's all right . . . can't play Chess though,' answered Suky.

'That's the whole point of the club – to learn the game,' I told her.

'Nah,' said Hannah, 'the whole point is to get out of late lunches . . . I don't want to learn how to play this stupid game . . .'

I smirked at her.

'It's not stupid though, is it? It's an ancient and venerable game of strategy and intellect . . .'

'Yeah, like, what-*ever* . . .' replied Suky in a fake American accent. Holding her hand out in my face.

Hannah picked up a queen.

'What's this one do?' she asked.

'That's the Queen . . . she's the strongest piece on the board,' came a reply from behind us.

We turned to find Wesley looking at us, pushing his glasses back up his nose. He was bright red but trying to hide his embarrassment with a smile.

'And who exactly asked you Wesley?' asked Suky.

Wesley shifted uncomfortably.

'Don't be so rude, Suky,' said Hannah, smiling at the poor lad as I tried not to laugh.

'*Poor Wesley* . . . why don't you tell us *all* about it?' she said to him.

'Well . . . um . . . er . . . it's the best piece. It can do anything . . .'

Hannah leaned towards him with her head cocked to one side, mischief in her eyes.

'*Anything* . . . ?' she whispered.

'Er . . . um . . .' replied Wesley, not sure where to look.

'Now, that's a game I *like*,' she continued – really laying on the dramatics and drawing out the 'like' – 'a game where the *strongest* piece is a woman . . .'

'I . . . er . . . I m-must get b-back . . . er . . .' stammered Wesley, turning around and fleeing back to his friends.

Suky and I nearly fell off our chairs we were laughing so much. I had tears streaming down my face. The lads had watched it all and they were shaking their heads.

'Man, you girls are evil . . .' laughed Jit, holding his sides.

'Pure wickedness, bro',' agreed Dean.

'Funny though,' pointed out Imtiaz.

Later that afternoon I was walking to my final lesson with Dean and Jit when Jit stopped to go to the loo. As Dean and I waited outside in the corridor he told me about some girl he liked in the year above us, Monica.

'She asked me out, man,' Dean told me, as a gang of older lads pushed past us. 'Watch it!' he shouted.

One of the lads, Marcus Thomas, turned round and

glared at Dean. 'You what? You gotta problem . . .'

Dean gulped and apologised, looking away.

'Didn't think so, likkle bwoi . . .' replied Marcus, turning and running off after his friends.

'You really know how to get into trouble, don't you,' I said.

'Man, I thought he was going to kick my head in . . .' Dean replied, with relief in his voice.

Just then Jit walked out of the boys' loo.

'You best go in there, Dean,' he said, all seriously.

'Man, what you sayin' – that I've *pooped* my pants . . . ?' answered Dean angrily, not understanding what Jit was talking about.

'You *what*?' replied Jit, confused. He hadn't seen the argument with Marcus. I grinned.

'Just go in the toilets bro'. There's something written on the wall that you better see . . .'

'What?' I asked, getting all nosy.

'Yeah what, Jit?' repeated Dean.

'Just go check it out,' urged Jit.

Dean walked through the door and was gone for a minute or so. When he came back out into the corridor he was grinning.

'Yes! The road to fame and fortune begins right here,' he exclaimed.

'What are you two banging on about?' I asked,

wondering what was written on the wall.

'Someone's written the words to the "Herbert Rap" on the wall,' said Dean with pride.

'Yeah and that means he's gonna find out about it and then you're in big trouble . . .' Jit pointed out.

'Rest yourself, man! He ain't gonna find out . . .' laughed Dean.

'That's really quite funny,' I said, giggling, as we moved off to our lesson.

'Me get famous!' said Dean as we walked into the classroom.

'You're gonna get killed, bro' is what you're gonna get,' smirked Jit.

'Shut up and sit down!' Mr Ashford shouted.

Dean grinned as we took our seats.

The next two weeks saw Imi, Hannah and Suky join up for a club every day except Monday. Exactly the same ones as Dean, Jit and I had joined. On Tuesdays we had Internet, Wednesdays was Chess, Thursdays Book Club and Fridays, Computer Club. It was really good fun, all of us being together at lunchtimes and the clubs were actually quite interesting apart from Chess which was just a laugh. And getting used to early lunch wasn't exactly hard to do. Even Imi and Suky who had argued the most when I'd told them about the socials came round and saw the benefits of joining up. I was just surprised that the whole school wasn't at it. Although that was probably a good thing because the more people that didn't know about it, the less chance there was that we would get caught out.

The thing was that no one seemed to care that we were all suddenly walking out of lessons ten minutes early. It was just accepted. The only teacher to raise a question had been Mr Herbert but then he was always suspicious of everything. And the morning that we all left his English lesson he had this huge pus-filled boil on his forehead and I think that he was just upset by that. I know that I would have been. Once I'd told him that we were actually going to a book club and that it was all part of our education in the English language, there wasn't very much that he could say really. He just grunted something about what it was like when he was at school and Dean told him, under his breath, to chill out and get some antiseptic cream.

'Or you might just get a heart attack . . . !' we'd all rapped on the way to the dining hall, laughing.

If we'd have known how things were going to end up I don't think any of us would have been laughing *or* singing Dean's stupid little rap. That stinky song ruined everything and I even managed to get some of the blame. Can you believe that – little old me . . . ?

FIFTEEN

Lunchtime heaven lasted for three more weeks before things started to go wrong. It was a Thursday when we began to run out of luck. We were all sitting in Mr Herbert's English lesson, clock-watching, waiting for the moment that we could leave to go to early lunch. Every minute or so Jit leant across and asked me what time it was and in the end I got so wound up that I ignored him completely. Mr Herbert was in a really bad mood and I didn't want to get into trouble with him. Since the minute we had walked into the classroom after morning break he'd had a face on him that my dad would say resembled a cow with a slapped arse. When he spoke it was through gritted teeth and he was all red in the face. Well, redder than usual anyway. As Hannah had once said, Mr Herbert hadn't been around when they'd passed out the good looks – he'd obviously been on the other side of the planet, running face first into parked cars or something, but she was sure that he had some other positive qualities, only we were still waiting to find out what they were. On that day his face was more screwed up than ever.

'He's got his face on inside out,' Jit joked in a whisper.

'Man must have constipation,' Dean whispered back.

It took all of my will power to resist laughing out loud, especially when Dean whispered that his granddad got constipation regularly, and pulled a face to mimic him.

'Serious, my gramps spent all his time looking like this . . . and then he'd say, "*Mi cyaan pass mi stool, dem . . .*" all the time. Even at the dinner table he'd be tellin' us bout his problem, droolin' an' that . . .'

'Ssh . . .' I replied.

'Serious – he used to say that his poo was all hard and dry and that and could my mum put extra hot peppers in him curry so that he'd stay regu—'

'Urgh Dean . . . !' I said out loud, regretting it instantly.

'Grace Parkhurst – perhaps you'd be kind enough to tell us what you're talking to Mr Chambers about?' spat Herbert.

'Er . . .'

'I should say you've *erred* young lady. Now shut up and let me get on with teaching the people in this class who aren't arrogant enough to assume that they know everything already . . .' he told me.

I went bright red and tried to think up clever replies but decided that the silly man wasn't worth it. He was probably sad and lonely anyway, and who was I to pick on him and make his life any worse than it already was?

Herbert turned to his board and proceeded to write out a list of points about something. I didn't know what it was because I hadn't been paying attention and I had to lean across Jit, who wasn't even bothering to pretend to write something down, and copy what Hannah was writing. It had something to do with imagery in poems.

I looked at my watch. It was eleven fifteen. We had over half an hour before we could leave for Book Club. I decided that the best way to pass the time was to actually pay attention which I managed to do until just past half eleven when suddenly a grinning face appeared in the glass next to the door and the sound of chanting went up outside the classroom, effectively ending the lesson. It was muffled chanting at first because the door was closed but slowly I began to make out the words as it got louder. Mr Herbert started turning purple with rage, trying to ignore it.

'*GEEZERS 'AVIN A HEART ATTACK...!*' someone shouted, banging on the door.

I looked over at Dean who was sitting with a grin on his face, and then Jit, who shook his head.

'Mi start a fashion . . .' beamed Dean, as someone opened the door.

Herbert shouted 'Oi!', his voice actually getting higher not lower. Some of the class began to laugh and you could see Herbert was about to go bananas.

The lad in the doorway ignored him and rapped some more. '*WITH YUH RED UP FACE AN DA HAIR YUH LACK, SOMETIMES YOU EVEN SMELL KINDA WACK . . . !*'

Behind him were three or four of his mates and they began to shout 'Big Up Herbert – an' da Herbert Rap, man!'. The object of their attentions started to shake and then he exploded, throwing his board marker at the lad in the doorway before chasing after all of them as they ran off down the stairwell laughing. Nearly everyone in class ran to the door in a mad scramble, Jit and Dean at the head, sending chairs and desks and bits of paper flying everywhere. I stayed where I was with Imi, Suky and Hannah, shaking my head.

'Someone's in big trouble over this,' I told the others.

'Yeah – Paresh Solanki for one – how can he just disrupt a lesson like that and think he's going to get away with it . . . ?' replied Imi.

We sat and waited for about five minutes before the stampede returned, picking up the chairs they had knocked over and returning the desks to their original positions. Behind them came Mr Singh and Miss Khan, telling us all to quieten down and get back to what we were doing. I looked at my watch. It was quarter to twelve.

'Miss Khan?' I said before raising my hand in the air.

'Yes, Grace?' smiled Miss Khan, who was the prettiest teacher at Devana High by a mile and also one of the nicest.

'Some of us have got to go at ten to because of . . .'

'Oh right, yes . . . those who are part of the lunch thingy can go now,' she replied before I could finish, saving me from admitting to the whole class what the gang were up to with the socials. After all, it was our secret and I wanted to keep it that way.

As we all stood up and some of the other kids gave us a few looks, Mr Singh raised his eyebrows at Jit and Dean, following them out into the hallway.

'What's this?' he grinned. 'You two going to a social . . . ?'

'Er . . . yeah,' replied Jit, sheepishly.

'What?' grinned Dean. 'It's Book Club and my mum reckons it's worth it for my education . . .' he told Singh.

'I'm sure it is – I'm just surprised that's all. Surprised and a little proud too. It shows great initiative lads,' Singh replied.

'Cheers, sir,' beamed Dean.

'What's going on down there, sir?' I asked Mr Singh.

'Never mind about that Grace – just get to wherever you're going to please . . .' he told me.

'Oh sir!' I complained.

'Goodbye Grace . . .' he replied, going back into the classroom.

'He's checkin' her – that Miss Khan,' said Jit to no one in particular, as we walked down the stairwell to the dinner hall.

'How'd you know?' Suky asked him.

'Singh and Khan? Man, that's just nasty . . .' said Imtiaz.

'Why is it . . . ?' asked Hannah. 'They're both about the same age and they ain't exactly ugly the pair of 'em – I reckon they'd make a nice couple . . .'

'Yeah so do I,' agreed Suky.

'What you two bangin' on about?' dismissed Dean, waving his hand.

'Hey check out what's going on over there . . .' whispered Jit, as we reached the main corridor at the foot of the stairs.

Across the corridor, in the opposite direction to the hall, stood Mr Black with Herbert, Granger and Wilson, all surrounding Paresh Solanki and his mates. The lads looked sheepish and I could tell that they were being lectured by Mr Black. We stood and watched for a moment.

'Move along please . . . !' bellowed Mr Black when he saw us, his face red from the effort.

We turned and headed in the opposite direction, ready for hot food and big-time gossip. The social itself was taken up with discussing the stupidity of Paresh and his friends. Everyone knew about it, even the pupils that weren't in the lesson but Devana High is like that – gossip takes no time to get round. We didn't bother talking about the list of five books that we were supposed to discuss, even though I'd read one of them and was desperate to tell the group what I thought about it. By the end of the club we hadn't talked about anything but the fracas during our lesson and I had to be content with holding on to my comments until the following week. Dean was still smiling as we walked to afternoon registration and continued to wear his silly grin into the next lesson. I think he was really proud that his rap had achieved cult status at Devana High. And you know what they say about pride coming before a fall . . .

SIXTEEN

The next morning we were sitting in Mr Granger's CDT lesson waiting for the time when we'd be allowed to leave to go to early lunch. Jit and Dean were doing their usual routine, winding each other and the rest of us up, as Mr Granger ignored them. He offered the occasional 'Ssh!' but nothing more than that, which was strange. Normally he was the kind of teacher that would throw pupils out of his lesson for being disruptive. He was showing us the basics of using a saw, and then began to go through the different types of saw that were available. It was an introduction to woodworking and to a project which meant making our own spatulas. I was actually quite interested and every so often I nudged Dean, who was sitting next to me, only for him to ignore me and carry on teasing Jit about a spot that had appeared on the end of his nose. He was getting his own back big time.

'It's like a new head, man,' whispered Dean, as Jit tried to cover it up.

'Get lost you wanker . . .' he whispered back.

'Any minute now the thing's goin' to start talking to me,' continued Dean.

Jit picked up his pen and told Dean he was going to stab him with it but Dean just laughed at him. 'You might wanna use it to bust all the pus outta that meteorite on your nose, bro',' he said.

'Why don't you just f—!' shouted Jit.

'RIGHT!' bellowed Mr Granger making me jump. 'I've had enough of you two . . .'

'At last,' whispered Suky. 'I thought he was never going to say anything.'

'Shut up and pay attention,' he told the lads, looking at his watch. 'You've only got five minutes before you go anyway – let's try and pay attention until then, hey?'

I looked at my watch which told me that it was only twenty-five minutes to twelve. I leant across, behind Dean and Jit and nudged Imtiaz.

'What time do you make it?' I whispered.

'Time you got a watch that works,' replied Imi, before looking at his own watch. 'Quarter to twelve.'

'Can't be,' I whispered back. 'Mine says that it's twenty-five to.'

'Like the man said,' Jit butted in, 'Get yourself a new watch.'

'OK,' came Mr Granger's voice. 'I've had enough of

all of you. Get yourselves off to wherever it is that you go to on Friday lunchtimes . . .'

I looked at Dean who looked at Jit, grinned and then stood up and made a big fuss of putting all his stationery into his bag. The rest of us followed suit and walked out of the classroom. I could have sworn that Mr Granger was smirking at us as we left. Not scowling as he normally did when he was angry. But once we were on our way to the dining hall I put it out of my mind. Why waste valuable brain space with thoughts of some stinky teacher and his facial expressions anyway?

The dinner hall was empty of any pupils when we arrived. The dinner ladies were behind the counter chatting to each other and waiting for the rush of squealing voices and cheeky grins. Normally there were one or two other pupils around, pupils like Wesley and Robert, other members of the lunch social elite, only I couldn't see them. Jit and Dean ordered their daily helping of pizza and chips and I picked my sandwiches. The other three were already seated, and when we joined them, Imi was complaining about Dean.

'I wanted to know what was happening in that lesson,' he told Dean, as he sat down.

'Sorry Dad,' replied Dean before stuffing half of his pizza slice into his mouth in one go.

'Seriously though,' added Hannah. 'Some of us actually want to learn stuff and it doesn't help when you two mess about and get us thrown out.'

'What you on about?' mumbled Jit through a gob-full of chips.

'Jit! Can't you talk *after* you've swallowed your food,' said Suky, disgust on her face.

'Yeah, that's just nasty,' I added in support.

Jit swallowed his mouthful and gave both of us a dirty look before stuffing a load more in.

'We ain't stopping you from learning,' said Dean, defensively. He actually looked a little hurt but Dean was a master at putting on faces so I ignored the slight pangs of guilt that I was getting.

'Yes, actually you are,' I told him. 'I mean – I don't mind messing about – none of us do – but sometimes you have to pay attention . . .'

'Yeah – you two need to think about the rest of us for a change,' agreed Imtiaz.

'Sorry,' replied Dean, looking away.

'Don't be a mardy boy about it,' Hannah told him. 'It's not like we're accusing you of something you *haven't* done.'

'Yeah but you're saying that me and Dean get you into trouble *all* the time – and we don't,' said Jit, after swallowing his food this time.

'Jit – you two are always getting us in the shit . . .' Imtiaz reminded him.

'*Yeah?*' asked Dean, aggressively. '*When?*'

'Like the time when you threw that *eraser* at Mrs Orton's head and blamed *me?*' said Hannah.

'Or the time you set *fire* to the text book in Maths with that lighter and we all got grief?' added Imtiaz.

'And what about that stuff with trying to get a free lunch because you said there were *hairs* in your food? You were pulling them out of your *own* head and putting them in the fish fingers, remember? And you blamed me . . .' Suky reminded him.

Dean tried to look hurt but his face broke into a grin and he laughed. 'Yeah but I was only messin' and that was *ages* ago,' he said through his laughter.

'We ain't got you in no trouble this year . . .' added Jit.

'*Woo-hoo!*' cried Hannah, sarcastically. 'You've grown up – break out the champagne . . .'

'Oh get lost *Hannah Banana*,' replied Jit.

'Wow! Haven't heard that one since infant school,' smiled Hannah.

Jit grinned and finished his food. Dean had already scoffed his and the rest of us had sandwiches which we took with us to Computer Club, the Friday social. On the way Dean boasted about how his 'Herbert Rap' had become popular.

'Move over Eminem, man. Ah me rule *tings* now!'

'You going to be in trouble when he finds out it was you who made it up,' said Imtiaz.

'How's he gonna find out?' asked Dean as we entered the classroom where the club was held.

There were rows of PCs and screens but absolutely no other pupils. I looked out into the corridor and saw no one turning up behind us either. Strange.

'Looks like we got here early,' said Jit.

'Come on, let's look for pictures of naked celebrities on the Internet,' grinned Dean.

'You can't, you little perv,' said Hannah. 'The search engines are blocked and anyway – this is a club for learning about how to use different bits of software – not the Internet.'

Dean tried to connect to the Internet but a message box told him that the modem wasn't connected.

'Man, that's so lame!' he said, opening up the paint box software and doodling on screen.

'What's that supposed to be?' I asked him, smiling at his inability to use the mouse like a paint brush.

'Your face, you cheeky monkey,' he replied, trying to draw out eyes, a nose and a mouth.

'*Charming*,' I said, pretending to pout.

'Why don't you try it then – Miss Artist? See if you can do any better.'

Dean moved over and I pulled a chair up, sitting down, and taking hold of the mouse. There were still no other pupils. I deleted Dean's lame effort and began to paint out a face, using different colours, watching Dean grow more and more mardy.

'Man – you never said that you knew how to use it,' he complained.

'My dad uses it every day – well, a form of it anyway,' I reminded him. 'And you didn't ask, did you?'

'*You're so clever – can I be your friend?*' asked Dean in a stupid voice.

I was just about to reply in a stupid voice of my own when the door opened and Mr Black greeted us with a beaming smile.

'Good afternoon pupils,' he said.

'Hi, Mr Black,' smiled Hannah.

'Now let me see,' replied Mr Black, smiling back. 'This would be your . . . Oh I guess this would be your fourth lunchtime social this week, wouldn't it?'

My mouth dropped open just before everyone else's did the same. I could feel myself beginning to go bright red.

'Shit, man,' whispered Jit.

'*Poo*, indeed, Mr Kooner,' answered the principal,

still smiling, as he was joined by Mr Herbert, Mrs Lee-Cross, Mr Granger and a very disappointed-looking Mrs Dooher . . .

EIGHTEEN

'It seems to me that we have a problem,' said Mr Black, sitting on a desk next to Imtiaz.

Mrs Dooher looked at me. Mr Herbert was wearing a self-satisfied look and the other teachers just stood there. I tried to hold Mrs Dooher's eyes but I started to feel embarrassed and a little bit guilty, like I had let her down, so I looked away. Jit and Dean sat in silence, heads down.

'Would you like to explain things, Mr Dhondy?' the principal asked Imtiaz.

'Er . . .' he began, trying to find the right words to say.

'How about you Miss Kaur?' asked Mr Black, looking at Suky. She turned her eyes towards Dean and Jit, saying nothing.

'We didn't realise . . .' began Jit, about to lie through his teeth at one of those moments when whatever you said needed to be the truth.

'Don't lie Kooner,' snapped Herbert, his face reddening. 'We're all well aware of what's been going on.'

Jit glared at Herbert. I closed my eyes and prayed that Jit wouldn't do anything to make things worse. I had this funny feeling in my stomach, the kind of feeling you get when you feel frightened. I began to wonder just how much trouble we were in.

'The funny thing is,' said Mr Black, 'if you hadn't stopped to gawp at Paresh Solanki's misfortune I doubt we would have noticed you. And if Mr Solanki hadn't kindly informed us of Dean's little attempt at hip hop, we might not have had a conversation about your little group.'

Everyone turned to look at Dean, who was squirming in his chair. I gulped down air.

'And had we not had the conversation that we did we might not have realised that you've been going to far too many lunch clubs,' continued Mr Black.

'Unfortunate coincidence,' smiled Mr Herbert. 'For you.'

'Although I almost *admire* your initiative,' continued Mr Black, 'I'm afraid that you *have* broken the rules and as such you will have to face the consequences. You know me – firm but fair, people. *Firm* but fair.'

Imi groaned and muttered that it wasn't *his* fault.

'Then perhaps you'd like to point out the person or persons responsible for this little episode?' snapped Mr Herbert again.

Imtiaz caught my eye and then looked at Dean and Jit. He waited for a moment and then shook his head.

'No – it was all of us,' he said.

'All of you?' questioned Mr Herbert. 'Not one or two of you leading the rest astray?'

'No!' burst out Hannah. 'We all got into it together . . .'

'*Really*? Past form suggests that there's usually a couple of ringleaders amongst you,' replied Herbert, looking at Dean and Jit with his beady little eyes.

'Actually,' I said, allowing the stupid part of my brain to win over the goody two-shoes bit, 'it was my idea.'

Mr Herbert sniggered.

'Forgive me if I find that just a touch incredulous,' he sneered.

'You even know what that means?' mumbled Dean.

'I'm sorry Mr Chambers,' replied Mr Black. 'Is there something you wish to say?'

'No,' said Dean, looking up at me.

'It *was* me!' I said in a loud voice. 'I told them all about it.'

'We all joined in,' added Suky. 'So it's down to all of us.'

Mr Black looked at us all and shook his head. Then he turned to Dean. 'Your form tutor will inform you of your punishment. And Mr Chambers, if you'd like to come and pay me a visit in my office afterwards, please.'

'But that's not fair . . .' I began.

'Oh yes it is, young lady,' answered Mr Black. 'Firm. But fair.'

With his motto still ringing in our ears he got up and strode out of the room. Mrs Dooher stayed but the other three followed the leader, as I wondered why the two that had said nothing bothered to come along. To catch one of us in a lie, maybe. Our form tutor closed the door behind Mrs Lee-Cross and turned to face us.

'You are a bunch of idiots,' she said in a soft voice.

'But Miss . . .' began Jit.

'I'm not interested,' replied Mrs Dooher. 'You've put me in a very tricky position. How exactly do I explain that six members of my form group all broke the rules together?'

'Ain't your fault, is it?' said Dean.

'No, Dean. From what I can tell it's yours,' she answered.

'Yeah!' snapped Imtiaz. 'Cheers, Dean. You've got us all into trouble again.'

'No one held no gun to your head, did they?' Jit snapped back.

'If he hadn't gone on about it,' said Suky, before looking at me, 'we wouldn't have been tempted would we? And let's not forget Grace either . . .'

'Oh go and boil your head,' I said, meaning to lighten the situation, only Suky took it the wrong way and went mardy with me.

'Get stuffed you cow!' she shouted.

'SHUT UP!'

We all looked at Mrs Dooher in surprise. I don't think that I had ever heard her shout before. I sensed that Jit was about to break into a grin and I desperately tried to get his attention by kicking his chair but he ignored me and smiled.

'Man, Miss is gettin . . .' he began.

'I mean it, Jit,' said Mrs Dooher shutting him up. 'You've let me down very badly. I thought that you all had more intelligence than this . . . It was a very stupid thing to do. You know it took the combined efforts of myself, Mrs Lee-Cross and Mr Granger to persuade Mr Black not to cancel all the socials for the rest of the year.'

'Man, that's just stupid,' said Dean. 'Why should everyone else suffer just cos we messed up?'

'*Exactly*, Dean,' replied Mrs Dooher. 'The socials are there so that you can learn new things not skive off lessons and get early lunches everyday. The clubs are an extra curricular activity. The school doesn't *have* to run them.'

'We know, Miss,' said Hannah. 'We *are* sorry . . .'

'That's beside the point, I'm afraid,' said Mrs Dooher.

'So what's he gonna do to us then?' asked Jit.

'If it had been up to Mr Herbert you would have had the book thrown at you but Mrs Lee-Cross persuaded Mr Black that there was an alternative . . .'

'What is it, Miss?' asked Suky.

'Yeah – what has this *fool* got us into this time?' added Imtiaz.

'Who you calling *fool*, pretty bwoi?' snapped Dean.

'*You*, you fool . . .'

'Shut it!' shouted Mrs Dooher. 'I don't care whose fault it is – all of you made a choice to break the rules and deceive your teachers . . .'

'That's a bit harsh innit Miss? It ain't like we killed someone and buried 'em under the tennis courts,' said Jit.

We all turned to look at him, the weirdo, and even Mrs Dooher nearly broke out a grin.

'You strange child,' laughed Hannah, shaking her head.

'Wha' . . . ?' asked Jit, shrugging his shoulders.

'It's a breach of trust,' said Mrs Dooher. 'And trust is a very important thing. Now you lot are going to have to re-earn mine and that of the rest of the staff.'

Imi groaned again.

'So, let me tell you what's going to happen. On

Mondays, Tuesdays and Wednesdays, for the rest of the term, you're all going to help out in the dinner hall, clearing tables and emptying plates . . .'

'NO WAY!' shouted Jit, getting a seriously dirty look from Mrs Dooher. A look that could kill. But she didn't stop to tell him off.

'. . . and you'll have late lunches on those days too. And on Thursdays and Fridays, you'll attend extra Maths tutorials, with work set for you . . .'

'For the whole term . . . ?' moaned Suky.

'Yeah – talk about overreacting, Miss,' added Hannah. 'The punishment is supposed to fit the crime, isn't it?'

'Let me finish,' replied Mrs Dooher. 'There will be an opportunity to shorten the period of punishment. If Mr Black feels that you *aren't* trying to slack off during the lunchtimes that you'll have to clear up, and Mrs Lee-Cross sees a marked improvement in your attitudes towards Maths, then they'll review the situation . . . in two weeks time.'

'Great,' snapped Imtiaz.

'Well I ain't doin it,' said Jit, sullenly.

'I'm afraid that you are, Jit,' replied Mrs Dooher, softly.

'But it ain't fair,' he said.

'And nor is what you did . . .'

Dean, who had been quiet for a while, slid his chair back and stood up.

'I'm going to see the top knob,' he told Mrs Dooher, not bothering to wait for her permission.

'Dean . . . wait,' Mrs Dooher called out after him but he ignored her, slamming the door in its frame and swearing at the top of his voice in the corridor.

'He'll be OK, Miss,' said Hannah. 'He's just letting off steam.'

'I know,' she replied with a tired smile. 'I just hope that he lets it all off before he reaches Mr Black's office.'

'We're really sorry,' I said, as much to the others as to Mrs Dooher.

'And very stupid,' she replied. 'Now get outside with the rest of the pupils.'

I tried to talk to Imtiaz and Suky as we walked down the stairs and out of the doors that led to the tennis courts but they both told me to go away.

When I approached Hannah, she told me that she had to talk to someone about homework and walked off towards a group of girls from her old school. Jit had gone off in a sulk too, so I sat on my own and wondered what I was going to do to make it up to my friends . . .

NINETEEN

The brainwave hit me on Saturday morning, as I stood in the checkout queue at Sainsburys with my dad, as he tried to find his wallet.

'I'm sure it's here somewhere,' he said to the man behind us, apologetically.

'Dad – I've got something I need to tell you,' I said, wondering if it was a good moment to remind him that he'd given me his wallet for safekeeping. It was in my little shoulder bag which hung at my side.

'Not now, Grace,' he said, as the checkout operator smiled at us and said hello.

'But it's really important,' I said, beginning to unload the trolley's contents onto the conveyor belt. As the bar codes on each item of shopping beeped past the red light, I opened my bag and took out his wallet.

'I think it might be in the car,' said my dad absent-mindedly. 'I'll just nip out and see . . .'

'Dad – it's here. You gave it to me in the cheese aisle because it fell out of your back pocket.' I handed it to him and put more stuff on the belt.

'Ah! There it is,' he said, as though it had just appeared out of thin air. Like maybe the air in his head.

'Dad . . .'

'OK Grace – what do you want to tell me?' he relented.

'I . . . we got into trouble at school yesterday.'

My dad smiled at the woman on the checkout and then turned to me.

'Who do you mean by "we" and what trouble exactly?' he asked. Looking worried.

'It's nothing much . . . just silly stuff and all of us got into trouble.'

'What – even Suky and Imtiaz?'

'Yes,' I replied. Even my dad knew that those two were perfect. Supposedly.

'And I thought they were such mature young people,' he said, trying not to smile.

'It's not funny Dad – me and Dean got everyone else into trouble and they won't talk to me now and I don't know what to do about it.'

'Can you start packing this stuff?' asked my dad.

'Are you listening to me?'

'Yes, Grace, I am. I just want you to pack whilst you talk, that's all.'

So as I packed the shopping I told him all about what had happened. Everything – no leaving bits out or anything. Dad didn't look at me once as I talked and when I'd finished he just pocketed his wallet and said goodbye to the checkout woman. Convinced he'd been ignoring me I went into a sulk. My dad saw me push out my bottom lip and smiled as he pushed the trolley, now full of shopping bags filled to bursting point, out of the store.

'I heard everything,' he said. 'I just don't know what you want me to do about it, that's all.'

'I've got an idea – something that I need your help with over the weekend.'

Dad raised an eyebrow.

'What exactly?' he asked.

'Something that will get my friends talking to me again and make up for what I . . . me and Dean got them into.'

We were at the car by that point and Dad patted his pockets, hoping to hear the jangle of car keys. When he didn't get it he started to look panicked.

'Damn!' he said. 'I must have left them at the till.'

Before I could reply he walked off towards the store again so I didn't get the chance to tell him that I also had his car keys. I could have gone after him. Shouted even. But I decided to let him go, smiling to myself at the thought of him asking if anyone had seen his keys and then thinking that he had lost them and deciding that he had to call my mum at home and get her to bring the spare keys in her car, something that had happened many times before. I got the keys out, opened the doors and started to load the bags into the boot.

'Very funny . . .' he said, grinning when he returned. 'Although your mother might not see it that way – I've just called her from the store and asked her to bring me the spares.'

'You've got to call her back,' I said in a panic of my own. 'She was going to have a lie-in and . . .' The thought of my mum having to get up early after a really hectic week at work didn't appeal to me. She'd be moody and I'd get it in the neck for playing my trick. I was in enough trouble as it was.

'Only kidding, Grace,' he replied.

'*Dad . . .*'

There was a bunch of deep-red grapes sitting on top of one of the shopping bags and I plucked one from the rest and threw it at his head. He ducked and the grape flew on, straight into the back of some woman's head. I got into the car as she turned and gave my dad a filthy look. He smiled and shrugged his shoulders before getting in and trying to tell me off through his laughter. Then, on the way home I filled him in on my idea to save myself and the others from lunchtime hell.

* * *

Dean was standing at the bus stop the following Monday morning as my dad pulled up to the curb. I lowered the window and told him to get in.

'So what – we getting chauffeur driven to school today?' he asked, opening a door and getting in.

It was a cold morning and Dean shivered as the car heater warmed him up.

'Thanks Mr Parkhurst,' he said.

'It's totally *cool*, bro',' replied my dad, trying, yet *again*, to act like he was twenty-five again.

'Dad!' I said, giggling.

I was well past getting embarrassed by him. He *had* helped me to turn my idea into something more concrete and he *was* coming into school to argue my case with Mr Black too. I could allow him to be an old hippie trying to be down with the youth for one morning at least.

'Nah Grace,' laughed Dean. 'Mr Parkhurst is cool man.'

'Thanks Dean,' beamed my dad as he turned up the latest hip hop CD that *I'd* told him to buy.

'Wicked . . .' grinned Dean. 'Man could get *used* to this, y'know.'

'I don't think so,' I said.

'You got that thing you were telling me about on the

phone?' asked Dean, remembering what I'd told him on Sunday.

'Yeah it's in my bag.'

I opened my bag and gave him a look at my brainchild.

'*Yes, Sister Gee – ah you dat, man,*' said Dean, nodding his head to the beat coming from the CD player.

I think he was trying to say I was clever or talented or something but I didn't actually know. And I was too cool to admit that sometimes I didn't have a clue what he was on about. He'd only tease me forever if I did.

Mr Black was at the front gate as my dad walked us both in.

'Ah Mr Parkhurst – good morning,' beamed Mr Black. 'And good morning to you two – bright and early, I see.'

'Good morning, Mr Black,' replied my dad.

'Hi, sir,' I said.

Dean mumbled a quick hello and shot off towards the doors.

'Do we have a meeting scheduled, Mr Parkhurst?' asked my principal, looking confused.

'No – we don't. I'm here on the off-chance that you can spare me half an hour or so of your *valuable* time.'

'A school matter?' asked Mr Black.

'Yes,' my dad told him.

'Of course, sir. How can I be of service?'

For a moment I thought that he was going to bow or something but he didn't. He asked my dad to go and take a seat in reception, and that he'd be along in a minute or two. I walked my dad into the foyer and signed him in before taking him to the waiting area outside Mr Black's huge, untidy office. I sat down with him and watched the other pupils go by, all of them staring at my dad and me, wondering what was going on. Usually when someone's parents sat with them outside the principal's office, they were in serious trouble, or pregnant, or about to be expelled. I wondered what the rumours would be about me.

About five minutes after we had sat down, Mr Black walked up, his infamous detention list clipped to the board that hung at his side. He grinned at me and told me that he'd take it from there and told me to get off to registration.

'Oh, I'm sorry,' smiled Dad. 'I forgot to say that Grace would be joining us. That's not a problem, is it?'

'Not at all, Mr Parkhurst,' replied Mr Black, genuinely. 'Perhaps I can get you both a cup of coffee?'

'That would be lovely,' said Dad, as we were ushered into the office and asked to sit down. Mr Black lifted his phone and asked someone on the other end for three coffees. He put the phone down and then turned to me and my dad.

'So what seems to be the problem?' he asked.

My dad told him what we had been doing all weekend and then went on to explain that although he thought that the gang deserved to be punished, he hoped that it might be something constructive.

'Something firm but fair, Mr Black,' he said, without any hint of a smile, the cheeky monkey.

'I totally agree and you say that you've prepared one in advance?' asked Mr Black, his eyes gleaming with what looked like excitement.

'Yes!' I chirped up for the first time, feeling more confident. I opened my bag and got out my brainchild, handing it to Mr Black. He looked amazed.

'And this can be done using ordinary software?'

'Yes,' replied Dad. 'Software that I'm going to donate to the school as a show of goodwill . . .'

'And you're willing to come in and train the students and staff on usage, troubleshooting, that sort of thing . . . ?'

'Absolutely. I thought maybe four lunchtimes this week – perhaps beginning tomorrow?'

'Marvellous!' bellowed Mr Black. 'If only some of the other parents were able to show such an interest . . .'

'So you'll let us do this *instead*?' I asked him, wanting to be sure.

'Absolutely, Grace,' he replied. 'Just think of the benefits for the school.'

'So we *don't* have to do the extra Maths and clear up the dining hall . . . ?' I said, pushing it.

'No – but I do think that you should forfeit early lunches. What do you think, Mr Parkhurst?'

'Call me Michael,' replied Dad, smiling. 'And yes I think that's very appropriate.'

He looked at me and winked. I winked back. Well you can't win them all and I *had* got the gang out of the other stuff.

'Perhaps Grace could get along to her lesson and leave us to discuss the details?' asked Mr Black, looking excited again.

'OK,' I said, kissing Dad on the cheek and thanking Mr Black again.

'You know my motto,' smiled the principal.

'Yes sir – Firm but fair.

'Exactly, Grace. And may I say that I admire your initiative.'

'Thank you, sir,' I replied, beaming as I made my way to what was left of my first lesson.

TWENTY

Mr Black waited until lunchtime to get us all together. I had a hard time keeping my secret to myself. I was gagging to tell someone else. Only Suky, Imi and Hannah were still mardy and not talking to me so that made it a little easier. And I had just as hard a time convincing Dean to keep quiet too. He wanted to tell Jit, who had spent all morning threatening to skive off when the dinner bell went. Dean didn't want him to get into even more trouble. In the end I made Dean keep quiet by promising that I'd make sure Jit stayed at school.

It was ten minutes to twelve when a Year 7 pupil walked into our classroom with a message from the principal. Mr Woods, our History teacher, read the note and then called out our names, one by one.

'It seems that you have an audience with Mr Black,' he told us, smiling. 'I wonder what that could be about . . . ?'

'Sack that,' whispered Jit. 'I'm outta here . . .'

Suky, Hannah and Imi groaned and got their things

together, trudging off to Mr Black's office without waiting for the rest of us. I got up quickly and followed, telling Jit to hurry up. When we got out of the classroom I told Jit that he *had* to come with us to see Mr Black.

'Why?' he asked, stubbornly.

'Because he's got something to tell us,' I replied.

'He ain't got nothin' to say to me that I'm interested in,' said Jit.

'He's letting us off,' I said.

'What?'

'He's not making us do the dinner hall thing. We're going to be doing something else instead . . .' said Dean.

'Yeah – bet it's even worse,' he replied, unconvinced.

'My dad will be there,' I said, knowing that it would change his mind.

'Your old man? In Mr Black's office?'

I grinned. 'Yeah,' I said. 'Come on . . .'

'But why is your dad here?' asked Jit.

'Patience, boy,' I told him, putting on a posh voice. 'It's not good to pester a lady for her secrets. And I *am* a *lady* . . .'

'This better be good,' replied Jit.

'Shut up you girl and get a move on,' Dean told him.

As we walked into Mr Black's office, the others were waiting for us, looking moody. My dad was sitting where

I had left him, a cup of coffee in front of him on Mr Black's desk and a couple of sheets of notes too. Mr Black waited for me to close the door before he spoke.

'Well, it seems as though you've had a slight reprieve,' he told us.

'I don't understand,' said Hannah.

'I . . . we've decided to give you something else to do during the dinner hour,' continued Mr Black, acknowledging my dad.

Suky and Imi both gave me a funny look. I smiled at them.

'Rather than make you do what I proposed on Friday, I've been convinced to let you participate in a little school history. From tomorrow Mr Parkhurst is going to use the lunch hour to instruct you all on the usage of a piece of design software, in order that you can produce, monthly . . .'

He coughed for effect and went over to his desk to pick up my brainchild. Turning round he showed it to the others. Hannah gasped and Suky and Imtiaz just looked at each other.

'. . . *The Devana High Telegraph*. Our own school newspaper.'

He held out the four page newspaper that my dad and I had put together over the weekend.

'But . . .' began Jit.

'But nothing, young man. You will participate or you will carry out the previous punishment . . .'

'No, it ain't that,' said Jit. 'I just don't get it. What about punishing us . . . ?'

'Well you will have to go for late lunch for the rest of the term,' answered Mr Black, 'so there is still an element of punishment. It's just that I've been convinced to give all of you a second chance. A chance to contribute to this school and to give something to its pupils. I should think that you'd all be very pleased.'

Hannah looked at me and grinned.

'Thank you, sir,' she told Mr Black, and beamed.

'Yeah,' agreed Imtiaz. 'Thanks, sir.'

'Don't thank me, people. It was all Grace's idea and she was helped by her father. If you're going to thank anyone it should be them.'

'And Dean,' I told them. 'Dean helped me with it too.'

I looked at my dad and winked on the sly. Dean looked confused but he didn't bother to point out my little white lie. He just scratched his head and then smiled a bit.

'It won't be a chance to skive, mind,' added Mr Black. 'You'll be supervised and I expect to see the paper go from strength to strength over the coming year. And of course I'll expect you all to train other pupils too . . .'

I stood where I was and smiled a big, fat, wide smile as Mr Black outlined what he wanted in the paper. Soon the others were all asking him questions and telling my dad about stuff that they thought should go into the first issue. Imi and Dean wanted to do a sports section and Suky asked if she could write a gossip column. Hannah applied for the post of editor and writer-in-chief, cementing her status as bum-lick by offering to do the first feature on Mr Black himself. The beaming smile that he gave her suggested that he thought it was an excellent idea.

'You know,' Dean said to him as we left his office to go for lunch, 'you're all right really. Like people say that you're *too* strict and that but I reckon you is OK, man. Firm but fair, know what I mean . . . ?'

The grin on Dean's face went from ear to ear and Mr Black grinned back, either not getting that Dean was having a joke at his expense, or just not caring. We went off to lunch and Suky, Imtiaz and Hannah all said they were sorry as we stood in the queue for soggy sandwiches. I told them that I was cool with it all and really looking forward to starting on the newspaper. We collected our excuse for lunches and went to sit down, followed by Dean and Jit.

'You're dad's really lovely,' said Suky. 'Helping us all out like that . . .'

'Are you kidding?' I replied. 'The minute I told him that I needed his help to design a newspaper he dragged me off to get the correct software package and a teach-yourself manual. He's nuts. Lovely. But totally nuts.'

Dean and Jit joined us and began to shovel the food down as usual.

'Man these chips are like concrete,' grinned Dean.

'Pure nasty,' agreed Jit, picking a chip up and throwing it over his head, not looking to see who was behind him.

'Oi!' came a familiar high pitched shout. It was Mr Herbert.

Dean and Jit didn't move. They carried on eating and talking as though Mr Herbert didn't exist.

'I'm talking to you two,' he shouted.

Jit turned round and smiled at him.

'What?' he asked.

'Did you just throw this chip at me?' asked Herbert.

'No,' replied Jit, still smiling.

'Well, *someone* did.'

'Did you *see* me throw a chip?' asked Jit.

'That's not the point, is it?' said Mr Herbert.

'Maybe it fell from the sky?' said Dean.

'Yeah – out of that plane that takes all the Devana High leftovers to starving people in Africa,' suggested Jit.

Mr Herbert struggled to stay calm.

'And shouldn't the lot of you be clearing this mess up?' he asked, trying to change the subject.

'Actually,' I replied, 'Mr Black has given us something *much* more important to do.'

'*Ask* him if you don't believe us,' added Suky. 'He's in his office talking to Grace's *dad*.'

Mr Herbert mumbled something and went back to his dinner as Dean continued to moan.

'Nasty food man. Concrete chips . . . there's got to be a way to get out of late lunches . . .'

We all stopped what we were doing and looked at him.

'What?' he asked.

'Shut up, Dean!' we all said together.

'Maybe there's another way out of it . . .' he continued.

One by one we all stood up and cleared our places, leaving Dean sitting on his own. But he didn't join us. Instead he turned to some girls from a different class in our year and started on them.

'Now ladies . . . Don't you think that it's unfair that we have to eat cold food and that . . . ?'

I giggled at him on my way out of the hall. Stinky boy. Jit came up beside me and asked me what I was doing later.

'Nothing – why don't you come over and we can have a snog,' I said, joking.

Jit looked startled. 'Relax, I was only kidding,' I added.

'Yeah until you get to Year 10,' said Hannah, winking at me.

'You what?' asked Jit.

'Nothing . . .' I replied, kicking Hannah gently on the shin.

'Oi . . . !'

'Oh shut up you girl . . .' I said, smiling.

Jit looked at us both and shook his head. I smiled sweetly and linked arms with Hannah. Then we skipped out onto the tennis courts together as Jit looked on.

Maybe I'll snog him in Year 10, I thought to myself, as I skipped along. *Maybe. If* he's wearing his lucky pants that is . . .